Warping sniggle porcupine salad...

It had taken me a while to put the clues together, but at last I figured it out and was trying to bring my assistant up to speed. That's when the case took another shocking twist. In the middle of my lecture on Poisons and Potions, I glanced around and saw that HE HAD FALLEN ASLEEP!

We're talking about conked out, unconscious, in a comatose state: snoring, wheezing, honking, and squeaking, the whole biscuit with butter and jelly. It took me only seconds to put the clues together and come up with a dialysis: *Drover had also come in contact with the poison*!

The Secret Sleeping Powder Files

HANK

THE COWDOG

John R. Erickson

Illustrations by Nicolette G. Earley
in the style of Gerald L. Holmes

Maverick Books, Inc.

MAVERICK BOOKS, INC.
Published by Maverick Books, Inc.
P.O. Box 549, Perryton, TX 79070
Phone: 806.435.7611
www.hankthecowdog.com

First published in the United States of America by Maverick Books, Inc. 2023.

1 3 5 7 9 10 8 6 4 2

Copyright © John R. Erickson, 2023

All rights reserved

LIBRARY OF CONGRESS CONTROL NUMBER: 2023944453

978-1-59188-180-3 (paperback); 978-1-59188-280-0 (hardcover)

Hank the Cowdog® is a registered trademark of John R. Erickson.

Printed in the United States of America

This book is dedicated to the people who lost homes, dreams, and loved ones in the Perryton tornado of June 14, 2023.

CONTENTS

CONTENTS

CHAPTER ONE

The Mystery Begins

I t's me again, Hank the Cowdog. There's a lot about this story that I can't reveal. Half of the Sleeping Powder Files are classified Top Secret and the other half is too scary to report.

You know how I am about the kids. They don't need to know all the scary stuff that goes on around here.

On the other hand, if we can't talk about either half of the story, that creates a problem. What's left to talk about?

See, every story consists of two halves, the first half and the second half. If there's a third half, we don't know about it and can't talk about that one either.

Here, let's go to the blackboard and see what

1

it looks like in the language of higher mathematics:

$$0 + 0 = 0$$

Or we can write it this way:

$$0 \ (\text{Half 1}) + 0 \ (\text{Half 2}) = 0 \ (\text{Story}).$$

Wow, is this cool or what? How many ranch dogs plan their daily lives around heavy-duty math? Not many. Most mutts don't think beyond squirting the next bush. Me? I mark the bush and go on to higher thoughts.

To tell you the truth, I get a kick out of playing around with big numbers...although, when you think about it, zero isn't exactly a big number. In fact...never mind.

The point is that we're facing a heavy choice. We either sit here like bumps on a log or open up the files enough to squeak out a story. As you know, I have an active mind and get bored pretty fast and being a bump on a log isn't very appealing.

Hencely, telling a zero story isn't an option. We'll have to declassify enough of the Sleeping Powder Files to tell at least part of the story, but be warned. It might contain some spooky information about spies and Charlie Monsters, and some shocking revelations about Sally May's rotten little cat. See, he went missing.

Should we take the risk? I agree, let's do it. If it gets too scary, raise your hand and we'll shut 'er down.

Actually, I don't mind exposing dirt about the cat. In fact, I enjoy it.

Have we discussed My Position on Cats? Maybe not. I don't like 'em, never have, and I especially don't like the one who lives on this ranch: Pete, Mister Never Sweat. The little creep.

One of these days, he will pay.

Where were we? Oh yes, we were in the Security Division's locked vault, sifting through stacks of Top Secret documents and hoping to extract enough information to make a story. Maybe we can pull it off.

Let's start at the beginning. Some dogs start a story in the middle and work backwards. Not me. I always start my story at the beginning because *beginnings begin*.

Middles...I don't know what middles do. Maybe middles muddle and that's no way to run a ranch or tell a story. I'm Head of Ranch Security and we don't muddle.

Okay, it was August, as I recall. Yes August, hot and dry, dry and hot, the ugliest month of the year. We dogs were sick of scorching temperatures and brown grass but there wasn't much we could do about it.

We can't move months around, you know. If

we could, we would, but we can't. Months belong to time and time doesn't listen to anything a dog has to say.

Neither do cowboys or ranch wives, but let's don't get started on that.

The point is that we had August, ready or not. For weeks, I'd been pulling two shifts every day and it had just about worn me down to dust. The work never ends around here. Sometimes I get so worn out, I have to use little tricks to stay awake: snap at flies, lick my paw, scratch an itchy spot.

I know, it sounds silly, but a dog in my position has to stay alert.

Have I mentioned that I'm Head of Ranch Security? I am. It's a very important position and sleeping on the job is a big No-No. If I took naps during business hours, I'd be setting a terrible example for my staff.

Drover doesn't need any bad examples. He is one.

So, yes, I was fighting against the tug bug of beeping sneep sloshing snorkles...against the tug of sleep, shall we say. It was tough. Something had bonk wronk with my flies...gone wrong with my eyes. The lids had become berry hominy... very heavy and kept frying to snork bonk...kept trying to slam shut.

When that hoppings, darkness markless

4

pudding and pie, and the next thing you know, warping sniggle porcupine salad in the sparkling whickerbills zzzzzzzzzzzzzzzzzzzz.

I was crawling through a dark tunnel, following the trail of a bone, when suddenly I heard a voice: "Hank, you'd better wake up."

Did you hear that? It was a voice but I couldn't see anyone, nothing but black dark. Wait, hold everything. My eyes had slammed shut. I'd been trying to keep them open but...

I had to try something else. What if I slipped a high-lift jack under one eyelid and pried it open? That might work. I slipped the jack into place and pushed down on the lever.

Crank, crank, crank. Light poured in through the croak and almost blendered me...poured in through the crack and almost blinded me, but I had to keep working.

I moved the jack to the other eyelid and cranked it open. The blaze of light was almost overwhooping but it gave me an important clue in this case: wherever I was, it wasn't night. See, nights are dark and they don't knock your eyeballs out.

I blinked several times and adjusted the fracas of my focus. That's when I saw...what was that thing? Someone or something was stumbling in frump of me...standing in front of me, that is.

I snatched the microphone and buttoned the mash...mashed the button.

"Unit One to Drover, over. Report in at once."

I heard his voice crackling over the speakers. "Unit Two to Hank, reporting in at once, over."

"Oh, good. What's your Forty-Twenty?"

"My blood pressure?"

"No, your Forty-Twenty."

"What's that?"

"Your location. We're talking on a secured connection and using code."

"I'll be derned. I had a code last weeg and by dose was all stobbed ub."

"Never mind your nose. What's your location? Over."

"Well, let's see. I'm right here and by dose is with be."

"Okay, do you see some kind of animal, maybe a dog?"

"Oh yes, I see one."

"Give me a Twenty-Eleven. Over."

"What's that?"

"A description, you goose, give me a description of the suspect."

"Well, let's see here. He's sprawled out in front of the machine shed and he's been asleep for two hours."

"Roger that, but the suspect I'm seeing isn't sprawled out and he isn't asleep. He's standing right in front of me, staring. Any idea who it might be?"

"Oh yeah, that's me."

His words sent ripples through the whipples of my mind. I sat up and narrowed my eyes against the glaring light of the sun and studied the figure in front of me. "You're Drover?"

"Yeah, Drover with a D. Hi."

"You work for the Security Division?"

"Yep, that's me."

"Where are we? What's going on around here?"

"Well, we're in front of the machine shed and I don't know what's going on."

I jacked myself up to a standing position and took a few steps. "Drover, something's wrong with my legs. There must have been an explosion."

"No, you've been asleep."

"I have NOT been asleep. I remember very distinkingly that I was trying to stay awake."

"I guess that flopped."

"I was in a dark tunnel, following a bone, but then..." I glanced around and tried to shake the vapors out of my head. "Wait, it's coming back now. My eyelids began sinking and I couldn't stop them from slamming shut."

"Yeah, it's called sleep."

"No, this was something else, something more snickerous."

"That's not a word."

"Of course it's a word. I just said it."

"Yeah, but you meant 'sinister,' not 'snickerous.'"

"I'll be the judge of what I'm trying to say and I'm trying to say there's something *sinister* going on around here." I paced a few steps away while snickerous thoughts swirled through my mind. "Yes, of course, it's all fitting together." I whirled around and caught him in a yawn. "Are you yawning?"

"Sorry. This seems a little boring." He yawned again.

"Stop yawning and pay attention."

"I'm getting sleepy."

"Yes, well, that's the whole point of this investigation. Don't you get it?" I leaned toward him. *"The cat has infected us with Sleeping Powder!"*

His eyes popped open. "Sleeping Powder! I never heard of it."

"That's why he chose it out of his bag of slimy tricks. He knew we'd never suspect it."

"No fooling? You really think so?"

"There's no other explanation, son. I don't fall asleep on my shift, never, yet I did. And now you're yawning your head off." I paced a few steps away. "Oh, what a treacherous little sneak! And I can

9

predict his next move. He'll start spreading lies and gossip about how we sleep all the time. He wants to sling filth on the reputation of the Security Division." I whirled around and beamed him a triumphant smile. "Drover, I've finally..."

Huh?

You'll never believe what I saw.

Amazing.

CHAPTER TWO

Drover Croaks!

Impressionable. Are you still with me? Good. This next part is pretty shocking.

Okay, you heard that conversation between me and Drover. Some of it didn't make sense because...well, Drover is incoherent half the time and I was recovering from a delicious attack.

A *malicious* attack, it should be. Delicious and malicious sound alike but they're not. They're very different. If you got jumped by a T-bone steak, that would be a delicious attack, because steaks are delicious.

I had fallen victim to a malicious attack, masterminded by the local cat. He had poisoned me with Sleeping Powder, to the point where I fell asleep on the job.

It had taken me a while to put the clues together, but at last I figured it out and was trying to bring my assistant up to speed. That's when the case took another shocking twist. In the middle of my lecture on Poisons and Potions, I glanced around and saw that HE HAD FALLEN ASLEEP!

We're talking about conked out, unconscious, in a comatose state: snoring, wheezing, honking, and squeaking, the whole biscuit with butter and jelly.

It took me only seconds to put the clues together and come up with a dialysis: *Drover had also come in contact with the poison*!

We'll never be sure exactly how and when it happened. Maybe the cat dumped it into our dog food. Maybe he infected our water supply or maybe he sprinkled the stuff on our bedding.

Maybe he did all three, just to be sure that he disabled the entire command structure of the Security Division.

I told you this was going to get scary.

I rushed to my unconscious comrade. "Drover, I've got some bad news. You've been poisoned but there's no need to panic."

Wow. He went off like a loaded spring, jumped two feet in the air, and began yelling and squeaking. "Help, murder, Mayday! Murgle skiffer poisoned pork chop, cranberry sandwich, help!"

He hit the ground, spun around three times, and ran smooth into the side of the barn. BAM! That put him down again, only now he was dog-paddling with all four legs.

I rushed to his potsrate body. "Drover, lie still. Struggling will only make it worse. You've been poisoned but that doesn't mean you're going to croak."

At that very moment, something very strange happened. *He croaked!* I mean, he made the weirdest sound you ever heard, something like the croaking of a frog. I was stunned. "What was that?"

"Help! I croaked, the poison got me, I'm gone!" He stretched out, closed his eyes, and quivered.

"Drover, stop this nonsense. You made a croaking sound but you're still alive."

"What makes you think so?"

"Because we're talking about it, you noodle! Frogs croak all the time and go on living."

"Yeah, but what about the ones that get smashed on the road?"

"They become pancakes of froggy tissue."

"Yeah, and they don't croak anymore 'cause they got croaked."

"Yes, but you croaked and lived to tell about it. Even more important, you're not a pancake."

He opened his eyes. "What?"

I moved my close mouther to his ear. *"You're not a pancake."*

He lay there for a moment, blinking. "I never thought of that. I guess that's good news."

"It's very good news. You're not a pancake and you never will be. You're a dog."

"Yeah, but dogs aren't supposed to croak."

"Drover, your body was under the spell of the

Sleeping Powder."

"Yeah, and so were you but you didn't croak. You snored."

"It affects each of us in different ways and we have different symptoms. Some snore, others croak."

"I still don't get it." He sat up and a strange light appeared in his eyes. "Wait, I just figured it out."

"What?"

He rose to his feet. "Frog rhymes with dog."

"Yes? Go on, what's your point?"

"Well, since they rhyme, it's okay for a dog to croak like a frog."

"Hmm. Are you saying that it would be okay for a frog to bark like a dog?"

"Well, that would be fair and we want to be fair."

I marched a few steps away, gazed up at the sky, and wondered...WHAT WERE WE TALKING ABOUT? Ridiculous rhymes about barking frogs and croaking dogs? He's not normal, you know, and he does this all the time, blabbering crazy stuff that turns my mind into scrambled eggs. Sometimes I wonder...oh well.

After a moment of deep breathing exercises, during which I took several deep breaths of air, I returned to his side. "Drover, this episode with the Sleeping Powder has disrupted the work of the Security Division at the very highest levels.

We must take counter-measures to cure ourselves of this plague."

"Yeah, I guess we'd better stay awake."

"Exactly wrong. We'll have to sleep it off and let nature take its course."

"Gosh, you mean..."

"Yes, we're going to shut everything down and take a long nap. We can't fight this thing, son. It's bother than big of us."

"Say what?"

"I said, it's bigger than both of us, and maybe you should clean out your ears."

"Sorry." He pounded his left ear with a paw. "There, that's better. I can hear you now."

"I haven't said anything."

"I thought you said we're bigger than both of us."

"Please hush and listen. We're shutting down the Security Division until we get these toxins out of our systems."

"Yeah, I'd rather be a Texan than an Okie."

"Exactly. I'll lie down here in the shade, you lie down over there. We'll beat this thing and come back stronger than ever, then we'll settle up with the cat." He didn't move. "What's wrong?"

"I'm wide awake now. I guess all that croaking woking me up, 'cause that rhymes too. Hee hee. That's pretty neat."

"Yes, well, here's a news flash. If you don't want to take a nap, you can stand with your nose in the corner. March to your cell and I'll start the timer."

"How long?"

"Two weeks. You can make up rhymes in prison. March!"

"You know, I'm feeling kind of sleepy." He yawned, went to his spot, and flopped down. "Nighty night."

"Don't croak in your sleep."

You see what I have to put up with in this job? They ought to be paying me double-dog food every day but of course they don't. They're too cheap and they don't understand...never mind.

I went to my spot, did the Three Turns Maneuver, and collapsed. I hated the idea of sleeping during office hours, I mean it went against all my natural so-forths, but this deal had been thrust upon us and we had to rumple mutter butter figgy pudding...zzzzzzzzzzzzzz.

I had a little trouble falling asleep—too many worries and cares—but eventually I drifted off. It was very pleasant. I could feel all the cells in my body, brushing their little teeth and washing their little hands, cleansing themselves of every particle of deadly Sleeping Powder. The natural therapy was working, but then...

Yikes! What was that racket? I was jerked out of sleep by loud banging sounds. Maybe the Charlies had launched an invasion with tanks and whistles. Missiles, that is, tanks and missiles. I leaped to my feet and grabbed the microphone.

"Big Dog to all units! Activate and load up your biggest barks! We've got Charlies inside the wire! Repeat: we've got Charlies wiring the insides and this is not a drill!"

Smoke and dust hung over the battlefield and my eyes were slow to sort out the...huh? Who was that guy? It appeared to be a tall, skinny man and he seemed to be...

Never mind, skip it.

He just won't leave a dog in peace and I don't want to discuss it.

Okay, I'll discuss it but you won't believe it. Remember Slim Chance, the hired hand on this outfit? He can't stand to see a dog getting a few winks of sleep. It doesn't matter that we've been working three shifts and staying up all night to protect the ranch. If he catches us sleeping...

This was beyond belief. The guy was wearing a devilish grin, marching around my exhausted poisoned body, and banging on the bottom of a one-gallon galvanized steel bucket with a wrench. I'm not kidding. Oh, and he was chanting:

"Arise and sing, ye lazy bums.
You can take your nap when the work's all done."

It was SO SILLY AND CHILDISH. Do other people behave this way around their dogs? I

doubt it, I mean, it's not something normal people do, but on this ranch...

I held my head a wreck...erect, it should be, I held my head erect and gave him a scorching glare. I wanted him to know that I was outraged by this... this outrageous display of childish mutter mumble.

He stopped banging on the bucket and smeared a grin all over his face. "Morning, pooch, only it's afternoon. I've already put in three days' work and you've put in three days' sleep."

Lies!

"I want you to know that this ain't a dude ranch."

Fume fume smolder burn steam smoke fire.

"We don't serve breakfast in bed."

Oh brother.

"And you need to pay the interest on your dog food bill."

Pay the interest on my...I glanced around to see if Drover was getting his share of this, but of course he had scrammed. The little goof had a genius for knowing when to vanish into the machine shed. He had left me all alone to face the rebuke of small minds.

I turned back to Funny Man to see what other nonsense he had in mind and...well, I was surprised. It wasn't what I had expected, not at all.

CHAPTER THREE

I Steal Some Jerky

O kay, there we were, Slim and I, in front of the machine shed on a broiling hot day in August. I'd been in Intensive Care, trying to recover from an episode of Sleeping Powder Poisoning, and we're talking about a serious case. Knocked out. Fighting for my life.

Slim walked up, saw me unconscious, and naturally assumed that I was just a dumb, lazy dog sleeping on the job. He always assumes the worst, you know. Then, being a shameless joker, he banged on the bottom of a metal bucket with a wrench, with the express purpose of waking me up in the rudest possible manner.

It worked, of course, and even did some damage to my eardrums. He robbed me of healing sleep and then I had to listen to his mouth as he made so-called jokes about me sleeping during business hours.

Never mind Patient's Rights or my years of service to the ranch. Never mind the sick and the wounded or the sanctity of an ICU.

It was very clear that he had crossed a line and had left me no choice. I would clean out my desk, turn in my badge, and resign my commission with the Security Division. If he thought I was a lazy bum, let HIM run the ranch and we'd see how that worked out. Let HIM bark at the mailman and squirt every tire of every vehicle that entered the ranch.

I lifted my head to a proud angle and gave him a look that said, "I can't believe you've done this," and began my march into a lonely exile. My future fell into shambles but his future promised to be even worse.

But then...he placed the bucket on the ground and sat on it, reached into his shirt pocket, and pulled out something that looked like...I don't know, a dried-up dead mouse or a strip of cedar bark. And he said—this is a direct quote—he said, "You want a bite of beef jerky?"

I stopped and stared at him. Beef jerky! Who or whom did he think he was talking to? Some common mutt who was such a slave to his stomach that he would forgive outrageous and shameful behavior? Ha!

He'd pulled this trick before, you know, buying my forgiveness with his homemade jerky. Well, his jerky wasn't all that great. He made it out of cheap cuts of meat that were...

"Usually I make my jerky out of a roast, but this was a special batch. I cut a sirloin steak into strips."

Huh? Sirloin steak?

He took a bite and chewed it up. His face bloomed into a smile. "Now, that's jerky, the way grandma used to make it. You want a bite?"

No. A dog has his pride.

"Are you sure? It's fixing to go into the shredder of my mouth."

No.

Sniff sniff.

Or maybe I would give it some thought, I mean, it would be a shame to...we shouldn't allow hurt feelings to rule our lives, is the point. Someone has to show some maturity and it's usually the dogs. We've been doing it for centuries, dragging our people down the road to...something.

Okay, I would consider his offer. Sniff sniff. No pepper. That was a positive sign. The last time we went through this, he'd loaded the meat with enough black pepper to weld steel and it almost melted my tongue. This time, he'd used a more dog-friendly recipe.

That was important. I mean, if a dog is going take a big career risk, he needs to know that he won't get his mouth burned off. It certainly appeared that Slim was doing the right things to end hostilities and keep me on the job, so...

Okay, I would renew my contract and stay with the ranch. I moved toward him and shifted my tail into wags that said, "Just this one time."

To which he said, "Sit."

This was silly but oh well. I sat. And waited.

"You don't get the whole piece."

I never expected the whole piece. The only time I'd ever gotten a whole piece of jerky was when I'd snatched it out of his hand. Could we get on with this?

"How much do you deserve?"

Well, since he'd put it that way, I deserved the whole thing—my share plus damages. I mean, he was the one who had created this whole mess, invading my privacy, banging on the bucket, and insulting my reputation.

He held up the jerky and studied it. "What would you think about...one-third?"

What? No! Stop being a tightwad and finish

the deal.

"Okay, we'll go halves...if I can cut it in two."

He parked the jerky between his teeth and dug into his pocket for his knife. He had to dig pretty deep and got distracted and...hmmm. I saw a brief window of opportunity. I was sitting there, waiting for a settlement, and there was the strip of jerky, clenched in his teeth, only a short distance away. Hmm.

I made some rapid calculations. Could I pull off a lightning strike? Maybe. Yes. But it would, uh, create problems on the diplomatic front, shall we say. Was it worth the risk?

Sniff sniff. Yes! He wouldn't need his knife.

I struck like a cobra and seized the prize in my front teeth. I pulled and he clamped down, and for a moment of heartbeats, we engaged in a pulling contest with our faces only inches apart. I could hear him making peculiar noises and he gave me a hard shove...and guess what, that did the trick.

Heh heh. It pulled the jerky out of his mouth and I got the whole thing. Slim got...well, an education about dogs.

1. Don't try to cheat a dog out of his share of the jerky.

2. Don't give a dog more temptation than he can handle.

3. Congratulations, here's your diploma.

4. Hee hee!

I chewed up the jerky and rammed it down the pipe. I think it was pretty good but it happened so fast, I really didn't experience much of a taste.

He was torqued. "Thief! I can't believe you done that."

Yes, well, that's the purpose of education, to fill in the gaps of what we can't believe.

"You liked to have yanked my teeth out. Hammerhead. See if I ever share my jerky with

you again." He smoldered and glared and muttered. "Just for that, I ain't taking you with me today. You can stay here and be fly bait."

He gave me an ugly face and went into the machine shed.

Well, it's sad when old friends can't work out their differences. Was one piece of jerky worth a whole lifetime of happy times and shared adventures? I gave that some thought and noticed that a wicked smile had moved across my mouth like a wave on the ocean.

Yes. Slim would get over it, I mean we'd gone through this before. He would pout and fume for a couple of hours, then he would forget about it and we would start all over. He never carried a grudge for long.

I took a big yawn and stretch. While he nursed his pride back to health, I would put my spare time to good use. Did I mention that we'd been working double shifts at the Security Division? We had. It was the Summer Schedule, long days and short nights, but even more exhausting than usual because of the awful heat.

In the punishing heat, I'd been doing Traffic twice a day, Child Care with Little Alfred, and escorting Sally May to and from the chicken house so that she could gather the eggs. Slurp.

Sorry, please ignore that slurp. Because of the hot weather, egg production had dropped off and the hens weren't laying many slurps, but Sally May still needed a Full Escort.

I was glad to handle that department, but it had taken its toll. Two long shifts in the heat will drag a dog down and we need to restore the balance of our bodily fluids. And don't forget, I'd been exposed to the deadly Sleeping Powder.

Hencely, whilst Slim tended to the little nothings in his cowboy world, I would seize the opportunity to grab a few winks of healing sleep.

I found a nice piece of shade on the north side of the water storage tank, did the Three Turns Maneuver, and collapsed. Oh yes! Every cell in my enormous body rejoiced and sang the "Jalapeño Chorus" and within seconds, I had drifted out upon the placid waters of the honk mork snurf.

Perhaps I fell into a light doze and dreamed. Yes, I dreamed but ...wait, is it supposed to be "dreamed" or "dreamt?" Let's take a closer look at that, I mean, we want to get it right. We have kids in the audience.

Dreamed...OR...Dreamt

Seemed...OR...Sempt

Beamed...OR...Bempt

Gleamed...OR...Glempt

All at once, this seems ridiculous, so let's skip it. "Dreamt" is a bozo word that somebody made up to confuse us. Around here, when we dream, we say we *dreamed.*

So, yes, I dreamt I was sitting alone in a dark theater, munching popcorn and watching the classic old-time movie favorite, "The Glorious Pooch," starring me in the leading role and Miss Beulah the Collie as the damsel in distress.

Wow, what a show! A big castle, sword fights, gaudy costumes, jousting, delicious love scenes... rain? What a bummer. It was raining on the show! Beulah's hair-do melted, my popcorn got wet...huh?

My eyes slid open and I staggered to my feed. To my feet, it should be. It was still raining! In other words, I had dreamt it was raining but it also WAS raining, but there were no clouds in the sky. What was going on around here?

That's when I saw a skinny, grinning cowboy, wearing a straw hat and a faded blue denim work shirt and jeans. Did I mention that he was grinning? He wore a huge grin and was holding what appeared to be...A GARDEN HOSE?

Never mind, skip it.

It didn't happen and if it did, you don't need to know about it.

Phooey.

CHAPTER FOUR

I Get Chicken Marks

Okay, you probably figured it out, so we might as well drag it out into the open. Slim Chance, our local comedian, had pouted for ten minutes, because I had snatched a piece of beef jerky out of his teeth.

Was that such a big deal? Had the earth stopped turning? Had civilizations crumbled into dust? Oh no, but it had ruffled his little pride, so when he saw me...hey, I needed the sleep. I'd been poisoned and working hard and ...I've already mentioned that but it was true. I was exhausted, worn down to a stub of my former shelf.

He saw me lying in the shade of the storage tank, having wonderful dreams that starred me and the lovely Miss Beulah, and he just couldn't...

something happens to the man when he sees a sleeping dog, I mean, he transforms into some kind of...I can't even describe it...some kind of devil or vampire.

He'd seen the garden hose beside a tank that held a thousand gallons of water and it tripped some kind of switch. He couldn't resist. He cranked on the water and you can figure out the rest.

I got drenched. It was an outrageous display of childish mutter mumble and I sprinted to the machine shed. Just before diving inside, I heard his voice. "Paybacks, Hankie, the jerky."

I didn't have time to make a blistering reply (the spray of water had followed me), otherwise I would have yelled, "I'm glad I stole your jerky! If I ever get another chance, I'll do it again. I only regret that I didn't jerk out a couple of teeth!"

Pretty awesome, huh? You bet, and did you catch the barb of humor? "Jerky" and "jerk out his teeth." Heh. When they get me riled up, my poetic senses shift into a higher gear. Next time, I would respond with words that would singe his whiskers.

But would there be a "next time?" Don't forget, this conflict between me and Slim had been raging for half an hour, and I'd been on the virgil of resigning my commission and quitting the ranch. Was this latest episode serious enough to end my career?

I gave that some serious thought and tried to...hmm. I couldn't remember exactly what had started all the anger and bitterness. Slim must have done something really awful, something bad enough to shatter our relationship, but what?

Oh yes, he had caught me sleeping, banged on a bucket to wake me up, then accused me of sleeping on the job. It was a shameless pack of lies that contained...well, a whisper of truth. Let's face it: he'd caught me napping, which is embarrassing to someone in my position.

What he didn't know, and couldn't have known, was that the cat had infected the place with Sleeping Powder, shutting down the entire Security Division. Hencely, whatever problems I had with Slim didn't amount to much. He'd accused me of sleeping because I was unconscious and appeared to be asleep.

The cat had turned friend against friend, pal against pal, and now he was probably laughing his head off. Oh, what a sneak! Well, this meant war and it was time to...

Wait a second, hold everything. I just remembered something. This whole mess had started with Drover saying, "Hank, you'd better wake up," but *he never got around to telling me why*

I needed to wake up. Could this be a clue that would blow the case wide open? I had to find out.

"Drover, I know you're in here. Report to the front at once."

"Is Slim still banging on the pot?"

"It wasn't a pot, it was a bucket."

"Well, it hurt my ears. I can't stand loud noises."

"We're way past the bucket, son. After you left, it got even worse. He sprayed me with the water hose."

"Yeah, and I hate water. I'll stay in here for a while, if that's okay."

"It's not okay. Come out at once, and that is a direct order."

"Oh rats." At last he came creeping out of his Secret Sanctuary, where he had been hiding from Life Itself.

"Sit." He sat. "Let me begin this briefing by informing you that five Chicken Marks will be added to your record."

"Gosh, what did I do?"

"When the banging started, you fled, leaving me alone with a crazy person."

"Yeah, it hurt my ears. And I was scared."

"You were worse than scared. You turned into a little chicken."

His head sank. "I know, it happens all the time. I can't help it."

"Maybe five Chicken Marks will improve your attitude."

He began to sniffle. "They won't help, it's too late. I'm just...I'm just a little chicken and I'll always be a little chicken!" He started crying.

This wasn't the reaction I had expected and it made me...well, uncomfortable. "Please don't cry."

He shifted from mere crying to *bawling*. "Who wouldn't cry? I'm such a failure and I hate my stub tail! Oh-h-h!"

His sobs filled my ears and I felt my anger melting away. "Drover, maybe it's not as bad as you think. There's always hope."

"Not with me!"

I heard his tears plinking on the cement floor. "Here's a thought. Maybe we could reduce your punishment to three Chicken Marks." He shook his head and bawled louder than ever. "All right, we'll drop the Chicken Marks. Stop bawling."

"I'm not bawling, I'm weeping!"

"All right, stop weeping and let's get on with our lives. We'll erase all your Chicken Marks."

"No fooling?"

"No fooling. I have the authority to do that."

He looked at me through tear-shimmering

eyes. "How come *you* never get Chicken Marks?"

"Huh? Because...well, there are many reasons. The main one is that I'm not a little chicken."

I guess that was the wrong thing to say. It brought more howls and moans. "See? Nobody understands what it's like to be a little chicken, because they've never been little chickens in their whole lives! I'm all alone and such a failure!"

Oh brother. I paced and waited for him to get the boo-hoo out of his system, but it kept coming. "Okay, let's try another approach. What if I gave myself four Chicken Marks?"

"How come four?"

"Well, I have seniority and don't need the full load." He bawled louder than ever and I had to raise my voice. "All right, all right, I'll give myself five Chicken Marks! Stop bawling."

He sniffled and quivered for a moment. "Can I see 'em?"

"See what?"

"The Chicken Marks, the real thing."

I heaved a sigh. "Drover, this is...okay, when we get back to the office, I'll open the files and you can see all the documents. On one of the spreadsheets, you'll see a column titled 'Chicken Marks' and it will contain the number 5."

"Under whose name?"

"Under my name, you little...why are you so suspicious?"

He grinned. "I don't want you to cheat."

"Fine. You can audit the books, snoop all you want. Now, can we get back to work?"

"Yeah, I feel better now."

"Great."

This was so ridiculous, I could hardly believe I was a part of it. I mean, giving myself five Chicken Marks just to satisfy little Mister Boo-Hoo? It was beyond crazy, but it gives you some idea of what's happening every day and night on the twelfth floor of the Security Division's Vast Office Complex. While others sleep and goof off, I'm chained to my desk, giving myself Chicken Marks, for crying out loud.

Incredible. I mean, Drover is a borderline lunatic. I should have fired him years ago, but I keep trying to help him along Life's Thorny Path. No ordinary dog would put up with such a mess. I do it because...I often wonder why.

Anyway, this gives you a glimpse into Life Behind the Veil, what really goes on behind the scenes at the Security Division, and you don't need to blab it around. It's nothing to be proud of.

Now, where were we? I have no idea, something that involved Drover. I paced back and forth and searched the misty darkness of my memory. At last, it came to me and I whirled around to face him.

"Are you yawning again?"

"Yeah, just one. Sorry."

"Stop yawning. Haven't you caused enough damage to this department?"

"Sorry."

"Drover, at some point in this day of chaos and folly, you stood over me and said, 'Hank, you'd better wake up.' Why did you say that?"

"'Cause you were asleep."

"Why did you feel the need to wake me up? Was it something important?"

He rolled his eyes around. "Well, let me think here." He lifted his left hind leg and scratched his ear. "It must have been important."

"Please stop scratching."

"Sorry. It helps me think.

"Hurry up."

"I knew you'd want to know, but..." His eyes popped open. "Oh my gosh, I just remembered. Pete's gone missing. He ran off."

"What!"

CHAPTER FIVE

Pete Has Varnished!

For a moment of heartbeats, I stood there in stunned silence, staring at the little mutt who had delivered this shocking news. Then the entire machine shed echoed with barks, laughter, and yelps of pure joy.

I found myself dancing and doing flips. "The cat is gone, oh happy day! At last, we're rid of the little pestilence! Life will begin all over again and it will be a wonderful life, perfect in every detail, nothing but flowers and rainbows!" I gave him a hug. "Drover, this is the best day of my life! Thank you for this amazing...but why didn't you tell me sooner?"

"Well, I tried but you were asleep."

My smile faded and I stepped back. "Drover,

we've already covered this. After a thorough investigation, a team of experts reached the conclusion that I wasn't asleep. I had fallen victim to an attack of Sleeping Powder, planted by the cat. You yourself became a victim."

"Yeah, but there's a problem."

"There's not a problem. It's an open-and-shut case. Just follow the science."

"Well, there's a problem with the science."

I gave him a stern glare. "Oh, you don't believe in science? Explain yourself."

He rolled his eyes around. "Well, Pete's been gone for two days, so he couldn't have done it."

A jolt of electricity surged down my spinalary backbone but I tried to remain calm. "That's absurd. We already know that he did it, therefore he couldn't have been gone for two days. Who gave you this garbage information?"

"I heard Sally May talking to Loper."

"Are you going to believe Sally May or me?"

"It's her cat."

I stuck my nose in his face. "And it's my ranch! If the cat didn't do it, then who did?"

He grinned. "Well, maybe there wasn't any Sleeping Powder."

"What! Are you saying..." I marched a few steps away. My head was swirling. "I can't believe you're doing this to me. We spent hours working on this case, we had it wrapped up, and now you're..." There was a long, throbbing moment of silence. "Drover, some cases are unslobable."

"You mean unsolvable?"

"Will you hush and let me finish?"

"Sorry."

"Some cases are unsolvable. We put them in the Cold Case File and go back to them in a year or so. This is one of those. I'm sure the cat did it, I know he did, but we don't have enough evidence to give him the thrashing he so richly deserves."

"Yeah, and he's not here anyway."

"Exactly. He's a very clever crook."

"Wait, here's an idea. Maybe there wasn't any Sleeping Powder."

"You've already said that."

"Yeah, and maybe it's true."

"Never fall for the obvious, son. The fact that there's no evidence is proof the cat was behind it." I paced over to him and laid a paw on his shoulder. "We'll bag the little sneak but it might take a while. In the meantime, we must keep this to ourselves."

"You mean..."

"Yes, Top Secret. If word of this ever leaked out, it wouldn't look good for the Security Division. Why are you crossing your eyes?"

"I'm all confused."

"I understand. I'm feeling a little woozy myself."
He yawned. "Maybe we need a nap."

I found myself...well, yawning. "You know,
that's a great idea. Sometimes the stress of this
job..." At that moment, I heard voices outside.
"Did you hear that?"

"Snork murk."

"Who? No, I think it might be Slim and Loper.
That would make sense. They work here, you know."

"Zzzzzzzzzz."

"Uh oh, there's a bee in here, so bee on the
alert. A little humor there, ha, but watch out for
stinging bees."

"Bees wax paddy whack give a dog a bone."

"I beg your pardon?" I turned and saw...he'd
fallen asleep, sitting up, in the middle of my
lecture on Evidence and Science! You know, there
are dogs on this planet who sleep all the time and
he was one of them. For a moment, I thought
about waking him up with a Train Horns Bark in
the ear but decided...no, let him sleep.

No, by George, he needed to be blasted awake!
He was on the payroll and had no business
sleeping in the middle of the day. This was
shameful. I drew in a big gulp of carbon diego
and was about to give him a blast when...his eyes

popped open and he said—this a direct quote—he said, "I just figured out the Answer To Life."

The air hissed out of my chestalary region and I stared into the empty holes of his eyes. "What did you say?"

"I just figured out the Answer To Life."

"No kidding? What is it?"

He motioned for me to come closer and whispered, "Banana pudding."

I pondered those words for several seconds. "Are you awake or asleep?"

"It's hard to tell."

"It doesn't matter. Sleep on your own time. We've got work to do, let's go."

Banana pudding. Oh brother. He's the weirdest little met I ever mutted, what else can you say?

We rushed outside to check out those two voices. Just as I had suspected, they belonged to Slim and Loper. They were talking and that explained the voices, don't you see.

SLIM: "That cat had everything a cat could want. Why would he run off?"

LOPER: "Beats me. Because he's a cat, I guess. Sally May's afraid the coyotes will get him."

"They do like to snack on kitties. Well, I wish him luck. He's on his own."

Loper gazed off into the distance. "It's more

complicated than that. My wife wants us to drop what we're doing and find her cat."

Slim barked a laugh. "That's funny. Two Great American Cowboys, chasing a cat."

There was a moment of silence. "Slim, I'm snowed under with income tax, got to get my stuff to the accountant tomorrow."

Slim's smile fainted. "Wait a second. Are you saying…"

Loper shrugged. "I had to make an executive decision. It was tough."

"You're going to sit in an air-conditioned house, while I'm out horseback in this heat, looking for a frazzling cat?"

"I hate it, I really do, but we can't afford to shut down the whole operation."

Slim shifted his weight to the other leg and slammed both hands on his hips. "Loper, words fail me. I've used 'skunk' so many times, it's lost all meaning."

"We all need to broaden our vocabulary."

"The vocabulary I have in mind wouldn't fit in a family magazine."

"Well, I admire you for holding back. When we use rude language, it makes us seem…I don't know, small and immature, I guess. Don't you agree?"

"I ain't believing this."

"But if it will make you feel better, the ranch will be a happier place if you can find her cat. Do you need help saddling your horse?"

"Dadgum right."

Loper glanced at his watch. "I'd better pass. This day's getting away from me. Let me know how it goes with the cat...and be happy in your work."

He waved goodbye and headed back to the house. Slim glared ice picks at him and yelled, "I hired on to this outfit as a COWBOY! Nobody said anything about chasing cats!" Loper raised his hand and waved. "Loper, you're a skunk-times-fifty!"

Well, I had witnessed the whole affair and knew that the ranch had entered a period of darkness. "Drover, stand by, Slim needs our help."

His gaze drifted down from the clouds. "Oh, hi. Did you say something?"

"Yes. Did you hear any of the conversation between Slim and Loper?"

"Well, let me think. They saw a skunk...and Slim wants to be a cowboy when he grows up?"

"No, absolutely wrong. Do you ever listen to what's going on around here?"

"Well, sometimes, but I saw a cloud that looked like an elephant. It was holding an ice cream cone in its trunk and trying to lick it."

"I don't care about elephants."

"Neither do I, but I love ice cream."

"Hush. Slim's having a bad day. We're going to activate The Sharing of Pain. Do you remember the procedures?" He gave me a blank stare. "Just follow my lead. The main thing is, look sad, desolate."

"That's a big word. I don't think I could spell it."

I gave him Fangs. "You don't have to spell it, sell it, or smell it, just follow my lead. Let's go."

I flipped a couple of switches and turned on The Sharing of Pain, the program we use when our people are going through tough times. It activates Sad Ears, Hollow Eyes, and Tragic-Tail-With-Slow-Wags. I turned up the volume and beamed it toward Slim. I guess Drover did the same, if he wasn't watching cloud-elephants eating ice cream in the sky.

He's such a...never mind.

Well, the SoP program was rolling and I studied Slim's face to see if it was working.

Keep reading, you'll want to hear this.

CHAPTER SIX

Things Get Complicated

O kay, there we were, Slim and I, standing in front of the machine shed on one of the hottest days of the year. Slim had just gotten some bad news and I had switched on The Sharing of Pain program to guide him through watered troubles. Troubled waters.

It's something only a dog can do, you know, a special gift that you'll never find in a hamster, a pet rabbit, or a cat. Some of us do it pretty well and that includes...well, ME, for example. I've studied and practiced all the techniques and got 'em down to a science.

I studied my cowboy's face to see if it was working. It was hard to tell. He looked...well, angry. He muttered, "Horseback in hundred-degree heat, looking for his wife's cat! I should have taken a job at the feed store." He mopped his face with the sleeve of his shirt and looked down at me. "Well, at least I've got a dog that understands."

Exactly right, a dog who would step up and share his pain. I would stick with him through thick and thicker, to the bitter end.

He gave me a pat on the head and scratched my ears. He even smiled—not a big one but it showed a glimmer of hope. "Pooch, I'd give you a bite of jerky, only you already stole my last piece. That's okay. If you didn't steal jerky, you wouldn't be much of a dog."

Right again. Nobody understands dogs better than cowboys and he was exactly right. Any dog who wouldn't steal a piece of jerky didn't belong on a ranch. He ought to be working in a poodle shop. Slim and I were tight-for-life, pals to the end.

"And Hank, I really appreciate that you've volunteered to help."

Huh?

"Help me find the cat, 'cause it's liable to be a long, hot, boring afternoon and I'll need some company."

WHAT! Wait just a second, that wasn't part of the deal. He must have misread my signals. What I meant to say was that I would share his pain *until he rode out into the pasture*. There, we would part company and go our separate ways. I had no intention of wasting my day, looking for a stupid cat.

I beamed him this clarification and turned on Slow Wags. I studied his face and saw...no change, he didn't get it.

This wasn't looking good and my mind swirled, then...wait, I came up with a great idea. Yes, brilliant, a perfect solution. "Hey, Drover, we've decided to give you a big promotion."

Huh?

He was gone, the little...nothing remained of him but several dog hairs drifting in the wind. The rest of his worthless little weenie chicken carcass had vanished. "Drover, you will be court-martialed for this! You will stand with your nose in the corner for a month!"

I don't know how he does it.

I turned back to Slim. He was looking down at me, still smiling. In a flash, I shifted out of the Sharing of Pain and turned on an urgent expression that said, "Slim, there's been a mistake. Yes, I'm a loyal dog and a friend to the end, but also very busy. I've got work piled up and really can't afford to go looking for cats. Maybe you over-estimated my level concern in this deal."

Would it sell? Could I head this thing off before it got completely out of control?

No. It flew right past him. He saw nothing.

"Come on, pooch, let's saddle a horse and get this mess over with."

Oh brother. I couldn't believe this was happening to me, getting shanghaied into joining a search party for my worst enemy, for crying out loud. I had only just begun to enjoy the peace and tranquittery of Life Without a Cat, and now...

We began the long walk down to the corrals and I fell in step beside him. This was an outrage! I would file a protest. But then, after we'd gone a ways, a thought popped into my head. I slowed my pace and fell a few steps behind.

Maybe he wouldn't notice if I, well, slipped away and dived into the machine shed. Heh heh. I mean, if Drover can do it, so can I.

His voice shattered my thought processes. "Hank, I've got eyes in the back of my head and I'm a-reading your little mind. Don't try any funny stuff."

Huh? Funny stuff? I had no idea what he was...good grief, can't a dog have a private thought now and then, without someone showing up with a microscope and a spotlight?

You know, it's a little creepy when someone

reads your mind. Sally May does it all the time but we expect it from her because she's a woman and she's got Radar For Dogs.

But Slim? He's a careless bachelor who studies grass and cattle and clouds but pays no attention to little details. You could turn a herd of goats loose in his house and he wouldn't notice. A dog feels comfortable with such a man, but all of a sudden...

Hmm. Maybe I wasn't as clever about hiding my secret thoughts as I had supposed. I needed to work on that. I mean, if you're going to have sneaky thoughts, you need to learn to hide them.

Well, I had been drafted for this job and couldn't get out of it—looking for a cat. Slim caught his horse, a big lazy galoot named Snips. Snips and I had never gotten along. I don't like horses in general and him in particular, and he didn't like me either. Given the slightest opportunity, he would chase me around the corral and try to bite off my tail. He showed no respect for me or my position with the Security Division.

He had all the ambition of a worm. His goal in life was stand around the corral all day, eating alfalfa hay and swishing his tail at flies, so when Slim showed up and slipped the bit between his big alfalfa-stained teeth, he was torqued. He seemed to think that working in the heat of the day wasn't in his contract.

It was funny, I loved it.

Slim led him into the front lot and threw a saddle on his back. Standing a safe distance away, on the other side of a stout two-by-six fence, I offered my sympathy. "You know, pal, you're looking a little porky. Getting your nose out of the hay feeder and working in the heat might do you some good."

"Shaddap. Do I have to listen to your mouth all afternoon?"

"Yes, but look at the bright side. I've got some great ideas on exercise and weight loss. Maybe we can pull off a few of those ugly pounds. What do you think?"

"Stay out of my way, mutt-fuzz, or you might lose part of that tail."

Since he was so interested in my tail, I turned my bohunkus in his direction and gave him a better look. Hee hee. I even wiggled it! Wow, it had a magic effect. He pinned down his ears, turned his head toward me, and snapped his teeth. It disrupted the saddling-up routine enough so that Slim said, "Hyah, hold still!"

I stuck out my tongue at him. "You were a little short on that one, Trigger. Bad aim. I guess you're out of practice and you've lost half a step.

Had you thought of switching your diet to wheat straw? It's got fewer calories than straight alfalfa and old guys need lots of fiber."

"I don't know why they keep you around. You're such a loser."

Hee hee. I know, it was childish, but I didn't care. Everybody expects the Head of Ranch Security to be stern and mature all the time, and most of the time I am, but once in a while a guy feels an urge to...well, to bust out of the old routine and get wild, do something reckless and dangerous—you know, walk up to the Bull of Life and wave a red hankie in his face.

A little humor there, did you get it? Red hankie. That's my name, see. Ha ha.

Anyway, heckling horses is fun but risky, I mean, the guy weighed twelve hundred pounds and wasn't kidding about biting off my tail. He'd never bitten it off but he'd put a kink in it a time or two.

I would have to be on guard today. Just about the time you think he's half-asleep, he'll come after you like an alligator on a deer fawn.

Maybe I shouldn't have...no, by George, dogs can be childish once in a while. I was heckling a horse who deserved to be heckled and I was proud of myself. We would just let the chops fall on the chips...the chips fall on the chipmunks...what is the old saying? We would just let the woodchucks fall on the pork chops...

Never mind, skip it.

Where were we? Oh yes, in the saddle lot. Slim pulled the cinches tight and, to nobody's surprise, Snips stamped his hoof in protest. Tough toenails. If you can't take a tight cinch, you're not a work horse. Find a job as a Shetland pony.

If Slim had been setting out to do normal cowboy work, he would have pulled on his special high-topped riding boots with the spurs attached, but for this job, he didn't go to the trouble. He buckled a pair of cheap spurs onto his work boots and left it at that. Since this wasn't honorable cowboy work, he wasn't going to dress up for it.

Ordinary mutts would have missed this. See, it was a kind of protest, a cowboy's way of showing that he was being forced to do grunt labor unworthy of a man with his skills. Cowdogs notice things like that.

Slim heaved himself into the saddle and paused to mop the sweat off his face. "Boy, it's hot." Yes, I noticed. He rode east, toward the machine shed. I fell in step beside him but kept a close eye on Snippers. He was watching and waiting for a chance to take a cheap shot.

As we passed the machine shed, I saw Drover

peeking around one of the big sliding doors. "Hey Drover, it's not too late to join up. It's a great day for a hike in the pasture."

Zoom! He vanished. He's so...

I had gotten distracted and Snips saw his chance for the cheap shot. He lunged at me and almost dumped Slim out of the saddle. I dodged his teeth and Slim gave him Double Spurs in the gut. Heh. Taught him a lesson, the big bully.

We continued east, into the Home Pasture, and rode around the north side of the house. At that point, we saw something unusual. Sally May had come out of the house and was waving for us to stop. "Slim?"

What was going on here?

CHAPTER SEVEN

Our Beloved
Ranch Wife

S ally May went to the yard gate and waited for us. We rode to her and Slim got out of the saddle. "Yes ma'am?"

She handed him a big glass of lemonade with ice. "I thought you might be ready for this. It's awfully hot."

"Yes ma'am, thanks." He took a big drink and smiled. "Oh, that hits the spot." He took another drink and offered me none, zilch.

Sally May seemed distracted, nervous, then she spoke. "Slim, I'm sorry to burden you with this job. I'm sure it seems silly but…" A quiver came into her voice. "Pete has been such a good, faithful companion. He's always here and always comes out to greet me. If anything happened to him…"

She bit her lip and turned away.

Slim's eyes and my eyes met, then he said, "Do you have any idea where he might have gone?"

She shook her head, wiped her eyes, and took a deep breath. "I can't imagine why he left or where he might have gone. I thought he might have climbed a tree, but I've looked and he's not here. Maybe I did something that hurt his feelings."

Oh brother. Hurt his feelings.

She sighed. "I guess we shouldn't get so attached to our animals. I'm sorry that you're getting dragged into my little drama—on the hottest day of the year."

Slim drained the glass and handed it to her. "That was good, thanks. Sally May, if the cat's important to you, he's important to me. No more needs to be said. We'll do our best to find him."

She smiled. "Thank you, Slim. You're being very noble and I appreciate it." Her gaze fell on me. "You're taking Hank?"

"Yes ma'am. His ears and nose are better than mine."

"He doesn't like my cat."

Yikes, how did she know that? Okay, history and radar.

"It don't matter what he likes. He's on the payroll, same as me, and he'll do his job."

She knelt down and took my face in her hands. We looked deeply into each other's eyes. The end of my tail began tapping, then she spoke. "Hank, we've had our ups and downs. I know you don't like my cat and sometimes I don't like you, but please try to find him and bring him back. Just for me, okay?"

A dog should never be put in this position. It went against every cowdog instinct and every rule in the Cowdog Manual...except one: No dog worth his salt will ever say NO to a woman in tears, even if she's crying over a stupid...even if she's crying over a cat.

This was a toughie. I summoned all my reserves of Duty and Self-So-Forth and set the tail on Slow Sweeps (I was sitting down, don't you see, and couldn't do regular Wags and Swings). I looked into her pretty eyes, which were still glistening with tears, and gave her my pledge: "Sally May, this is probably the dumbest assignment I've ever..."

Wait. That was the wrong approach. It was too harsh. I took a deep breath and tried again.

"Sally May, there are things about you that I will never understand but that's just the way the cards were dealt. The bottom line is that you're the Lady of the House and I'm a dog who's loyal

to his people. The fact that you're the one who delivers the breakfast scraps has almost nothing to do with it, honest.

"Therefore, I will undertake this crazy...I will give my service to this solemn crusade to find your...to find your friend, the cat, even though... anyway, I promise to give my best effort to finding your...choke...cat."

There. I had done my best. Should I seal my pledge with a lick on her cheek? Maybe not. No. I had memories of doing that in times gone by and it had always backfired.

I searched her face. There was a softness about it, a sadness in her eyes. She laid her hand on my head and gave me a pat. "Please, Hank."

Sigh. Okay, I was all-in, signed up and registered, contracted and pledged. I had no idea where this would lead, but a loyal dog can't say no to a lady with a tear in her eye, and let me repeat that scraps had almost nothing to do with it.

She rose to her feet and brushed the dust off her jeans. "Thank you again, Slim. I'll be waiting and hoping." She turned and went back into the house.

Slim's gaze and my gaze met. He didn't say, "I ain't believing this," but that's what he was thinking. A dog knows. I was thinking the same thing. Unbelievable.

"Well, pooch, let's go find a cat."

Roger that.

And so it was that we set out on our mission, under a blazing August sun. Where do you look for a cat that has gone AWOL? I mean, when you leave ranch headquarters, it's a big world out there. We had outside fences but a cat could walk under any of them, and probably would, just for spite.

Slim rode south, toward the creek. We stopped on the north bank and Slim studied the sand for tracks. My ears picked up a strange sound, coming from the north, so I barked.

Slim looked north. "Good honk, someone's coming, horseback. Who...by grabs, it's Loper!"

Sure enough, he was riding toward us in a slow walk. As he drew closer, I could see that he was slouched in the saddle and had MAD written all over his face.

He joined us at the creek. "Any luck?"

"Nope. What are you doing out here?"

"I came to help, what do you think?"

Slim chuckled. "What do I think? Well, I'd guess that when your wife went back into the house, she noticed that you were sitting under the air conditioner, pushing your pencil around while the hired man and the dog were out in the heat, looking for her cat."

Loper glared and said nothing.

"Then she said—now, this is just a guess, I might be wrong—then she said, 'You sent that poor man out in the heat and you're in here, hugging the air conditioner?'"

Loper glared and said nothing.

"You said, 'Hon, I'm the boss of this outfit.' And she said, 'Well, Mister Boss, how would you like to eat baloney sandwiches for the rest of your life? *Get out of this house and help Slim find my cat!*'"

Loper wasn't amused. "Do I have to sit here all day, listening to your new novel?"

"Heh. I was pretty close, wasn't I? Go ahead and admit it."

"Your day's coming, buddy, and I'm going to love every minute of it. What's the plan?"

"Well, you're the boss, you make the plan."

Loper slapped a fly on his neck. "We'll ride the creek and check the trees. I don't know what else to do. You take the south side and I'll take the north."

"Ten four." Slim turned his horse south and waded into the creek. "Kind of warm out here, ain't it?"

"Yeah, and your next paycheck might have a few deductions."

Slim looked down at me and grinned. "Good old Sally May. She kicked him out of the house.

Hee hee. He'll be mad for a month."

On the south side, we headed east, winding our way through and around the willow trees that grew in the creek bed near the water. When we came to a big native elm tree, Slim stopped his horse and ran his gaze over the limbs and branches, and called out, "Here, kitty-kitty!"

I don't know why he did that. Everybody knows that a cat does the opposite of what you want. If you want him to leave, you say "Here, kitty-kitty." If you want him to come, you say, "Buzz off, cat" and he'll come running.

Oh well, I wasn't bossing this operation and to be honest, it was pretty boring. It was hot and my mind began to wander. I fell behind and, well, paused to rest in the shade of a big cottonwood tree. Off in the distance, I heard...was that someone singing? Loper and Slim? Surely not. I listened closer and...yes, by George, my guys were singing.

The Dad-Gum Pampered Cat

One day in August we got word
That sounded totally absurd
To saddle up our horses for a job.

The boss's wife had lost her cat

Our orders were to ride and that
We'd better not come back without success.

The dad-gum pampered cat!
My shirt is plastered to my back
And sweat is just a-rolling down my spine.

If we ever find the little creep
It'll take restraint for us to keep
From cooking him for supper on the grill.

We saddled up and climbed aboard
Spurred our mounts and headed toward
The creek where her kitty might have gone.

The sun was blazing in the sky
The heat was broiling us alive
Our heads were brimming full of naughty words.

The dad-gum pampered cat!
My shirt is plastered to my back
And sweat is just a-rolling down my spine.

If we ever find the little creep
It'll take restraint for us to keep
From cooking him for supper on the grill.

The sun's about to roast my brain
This project's looking plumb insane
And keeping us from doing cowboy work.

We wouldn't do this for the king,
Or the president of anything
But Sally May...well, that's a different deal.

The dad-gum pampered cat!
My shirt is plastered to my back
And sweat is just a-rolling down my spine.

If we ever find the little snot
We'll show restraint because it's not
An ordinary cowboy kind of deal.
We won't be cooking him for supper on the grill.

Wow, what a great song! I couldn't have come up
with a better one myself. I was proud of my guys.

I yawned and noticed that my body was crying
out for a nap. I hadn't slept in weeks, you know,
and...huh? I heard a voice and it didn't belong to
Slim or Loper. Here's what I heard.

"What is that down yonder?"

"W-w-where?"

"Right yonder, open your eyes. It's got hair, so
it ain't a duck."

"Oh y-yeah, th-there it is and it's n-n-not a d-d-d-duck, a duck."

"Junior, that's what I said. It don't have feathers, so it ain't a duck. What do you reckon it is?"

"W-well, m-maybe it's a w-w-w-w-wolf, a wolf."

"A wolf! What's a wolf doing around here?"

"B-b-beats m-me, beats me."

Have you figured it out? I was sitting beneath a tree that contained two buzzards and I knew them: Old Man Wallace and his son Junior.

CHAPTER EIGHT

Buzzards

O kay, I was on a mission to find Sally May's rotten little cat and had stumbled into Wallace and Junior, the buzzards. I'd had dealings with them before and knew them pretty well.

They were perched on a tree limb and Wallace had his wings hanging open, for ventilation, I suppose. He bent forward and took a closer look. "Junior, that ain't a wolf."

"It l-l-looks l-l-like a w-w-w-wolf to m-m-me-me."

"Well, it ain't. A wolf has smart eyes. That one's eyes look like two holes in the sand, and the nose is too big."

They both stared down at me, which was a little creepy. In this world, we have two kinds of Ugly: Regular Ugly and Buzzard Ugly. Wallace and Junior belonged to the second category, although I must admit that Junior was a pretty nice guy...for a buzzard.

"R-reckon it's a d-d-dog?"

"A what? Speak up, son, you mumble your words."

"D-D-D-DOG!"

"Junior, you don't need to screech, I ain't deaf."

"Y-y-you n-n-need a h-hearing aid."

"What?"

"N-never m-m-mind, never mind."

Wallace narrowed his eyes and gave me a hard look. "You know what I'm a-thinking? That might be a dog."

"I t-t-told you, told you."

"The question is, will he eat? It would be some mighty good luck, finding dinner right under our tree, instead of us having to flap around all day in this heat to find some sorry little mouse."

A smile flashed on Junior's beak. "W-w-wait. Oh m-m-my, it's our d-d-d-doggie f-friend!"

"Doggie friend? Son, don't get chummy with your dinner. You know the rules: A buzzard's only friend is his next meal."

"I'll ch-ch-check." Junior turned to me and waved a wing. "Hi, d-d-doggie, y-y-you d-down there, yoo-hoo."

"Afternoon, Junior, how's it going?"

"Oh w-w-well, it's awfully h-h-hot and w-w-we d-don't w-work m-much in the h-h-heat."

"I agree. It's a good day to stay in the shade." Junior turned back to the old man. "P-p-p-pa..."

"I heard him. He ain't dead."

"W-well, he d-d-didn't s-say that. H-he j-j-just s-said it's h-h-hot."

"Junior, dead dogs don't talk, and it don't matter if it's hot or cold or raining on Tuesday. If he's talking, we can't eat him." Wallace craned his neck and glared down at me. "Dog, we're busy. Why don't you run along and bother somebody else?"

"Actually, I had a favor to ask."

The old man rolled his eyes. "How could we be so lucky? We're out of grub, it's hotter than blue blazes, and he's got a favor to ask."

"It's not much, just a small favor."

"Then you'll leave?"

"Promise."

He gave me a look that would have curdled milk. "All right, what do you want? And keep it short."

"I'm on a mission to find a cat."

"Hoop-tee-do."

"I wondered if you'd seen him."

"What kind of cat?"

"Four legs, whiskers, tail, kind of a snotty

attitude."

"No, we ain't seen him, so run along."

Junior perked up. "W-wait, P-p-pa, w-w-we d-d-did s-see a c-c-cat. R-r-remember?"

"Junior, hush. He don't need to know our private business. I've got plans for that little feller."

Junior looked down at me. "D-d-doggie, w-we d-did see a c-c-cat. He was l-l-limping, limping, and the c-c-coyotes w-w-were f-following him, p-poor thing."

The old man's eyes bulged out. "Poor thing? Son, I'll show you a poor thing: ME! I ain't had a decent meal in a month."

"A w-w-week, P-pa."

"Are you a-counting that snake on the road? Well, I ain't and do you know why? Because you cheated and got there first, is why. By the time I showed up, you'd already ate two-thirds of it."

Junior grinned. "W-well, y-y-you were p-p-poking ar-round, poking around."

"Son, I am the head of this family and I can poke around all I want. Daddies have a right to poke around without their kids," he stuck his beak in Junior's face, "STEALING ALL THE FOOD!"

Junior looked at me and shrugged. "H-he g-gets s-s-silly."

"I noticed."

"W-we s-s-saw a c-c-cat, cat."

Wallace roared, "Son, if we seen a cat, he's an investment in our future and you don't need to be blabbing it all over town." He whipped his head around to me. "Dog, as far as your concerned..." He froze and pointed a wing. "Son, lookie yonder what I'm a-seeing!"

We all turned to look. A roadrunner had just popped out of the brush. Have we discussed roadrunners? Maybe not. It's a kind of bird we have out here, a big bird with long legs, a long tail, and a tuft of feathers on its head. It runs around on those long legs, makes an unusual sound, a kind of buzz, and eats lizards.

This one had a lizard in his beak. He stopped, cocked his head, and stared at us and made that buzzing sound.

Up in the tree, Wallace was jumping up and down. "Junior, this is our big chance, easy money, free grub."

"Wh-what do y-you m-mean, P-p-pa?"

"Well, it ain't complicated, son. You're a big strong boy, five times bigger than that silly bird. Flap down yonder, beat the stuffings out of him, and steal his lizard."

"B-b-but P-p-pa..."

"Steal his lunch! Get on with it and hurry up,

first chance you get."

"Oh d-d-darn. Okay, P-p-pa."

Junior heaved a sigh, opened his wings, pushed off the limb, and flapped his way down to the ground. He made a rough landing and picked himself off the ground. The roadrunner watched, bobbed his tail up and down, and made that buzzing sound.

Junior gave him a smile. "H-h-hello th-there, M-m-mister B-b-bird. I w-w-wondered if I c-c-could b-b-borrow y-your l-l-l-lizard, lizard."

Wallace shook his head. "Son, this ain't a borrowing deal and we ain't beggars. Stick that left jab in his face, then come around with a right hook. Knock his block off, work him over, and take his lunch."

"O-o-okay, P-p-pa. I'll t-t-try."

Wallace shot me a grin and a wink. "That's my boy. Watch this."

Junior got into his boxing stance and moved forward. The bird stared at him for a second, then

lit into the middle of him, thrashed him with wings and claws, and drilled the top of his head with that sharp beak.

It was a short fight. Junior sold out and hopped away. "H-h-h-help, m-m-m-murder!"

Old man Wallace almost had a stroke. "Junior, get yourself back in there and...what kind of yellow-bellied, chicken-livered outfit are we running here! Grab my lizard!"

"Y-y-you g-g-grab it y-y-your own s-s-self!"

Wallace stamped his foot and fumed. "These dadgum kids! They've got no more gumption than an I-don't-know-what! No wonder this country is going to ruin." He whipped his gaze around to me. "What are you staring at?"

"Just watching the fight."

"Watch your own fight and stay out of ours. This is family business."

"Roadrunners are tougher than you might think."

"How would you like to have a buzzard throw up on the top of your head?"

I began backing away. "I was just leaving."

"Good thinking. Scram out of here and come back when you can't stay so long."

"Yes sir. It's been fun."

"Maybe for you, not me. I have to live with

that kid."

I hurried away, I mean, he wasn't joking about throwing up. That's what buzzards do when they get mad and you can't imagine...well, maybe you can imagine. Awful.

As I passed Junior, he was rubbing the knots on his head. "See you around, Junior. Which way did the cat go?" He pointed a wing to the east. "Thanks, pal. Watch out for roadrunners."

He grinned. "Y-yeah, n-n-no k-k-k-kidding, kidding."

Behind me, I heard Wallace's hacksaw voice. "Junior, this is shameful! You have brung disgrace to your poor old daddy and the whole Buzzard Nation, getting whipped by a frazzling skinny-legged bird, and I still ain't got anything to eat!"

What a pair.

CHAPTER NINE

I Find a Cat

Well, that little sideshow with the buzzards was entertaining but it had disrupted my schedule and I had gotten separated from the rest of the search party. Slim and Loper had ridden on down the creek, looking for You-Hoodie, the cat.

What a waste of time and effort, and we didn't even know why he ran away. You want to hear my theory? Okay, pay attention.

In the yard, Pete could get by with anything, as long as Sally May was around to bail him out, but the little sneak had one habit that made her mad. When she came outside the house and walked down the sidewalk, he would scamper along beside her and rub on her ankles. Every once in a while, he got tangled up in her feet and caused her to trip...and it made her mad.

That had to be at the root of this fiasco. Kitty tripped her and she screeched at him to get out of the way. It wounded his little feelings, so he sulled up and ran away from home, knowing that Sally May would be tortured by guilt. She had a sensitive nature, you know, and I could imagine that she'd been roasting over the fires of guilt, lying awake at night, and crying into her pillow.

It sounded exactly like something a spiteful, scheming little cat would do.

If you asked me, the ranch would get along just fine without him and he wasn't worth all the trouble he caused, but this rescue mission had been organized by Our Beloved Ranch Wife and we were working for her. Anything for Sally May.

So I munched on with the minchon...I mushed on with the mission, it should be, I mished on with the munchon...phooey. The point is that we had to find the little snot.

Boy, it was hot. I lapped some water from the creek and whilst my head was down, I noticed tracks in the sand...two sets of tracks. At first glance, cat tracks and dog tracks look pretty close to the same. Both show four toes and a pad, but closer inspection reveals a crucial difference: Dog tracks show *claw marks* and cat tracks don't.

I was looking at both.

My head shot up and water dripped off my chops. Do you see where this was leading? Remember what Junior said? He'd seen a cat who was being followed by coyotes...and the cat was limping!

Holy smokes, all at once the clues in this case came together. Don't you get it? Pete was wounded, limping, lame, dragging himself through the wilderness, and he was being followed by the notorious cannibal brothers, Rip and Snort!

A jolt of electricity crackled down my spine and went out to the end of my tail. I didn't want to feel sympathy for the cat...I did NOT want to feel sympathy for the little nuisance, but sometimes our feelings get pulled into a case, whether we want it or not.

Pete had overplayed his hand and now he was in a real mess, a no-joke life and death situation. Coyotes eat cats for a snack and we're talking about potato chips and pretzels.

A wave of sadness washed over me. The poor little guy. He was a pest but he didn't deserve this. If he got eaten, would I miss him? The Awful Truth hung over me like a dark cloud.

YES, I WOULD MISS THE LITTLE CREEP!

It made me ill to admit it, but there it was.

Okay. Okay. My heart was racing and my mouth was dry. Maybe there was still time, I mean, those tracks looked fresh. I didn't have the slightest idea what I would do if I encountered the cannibals, the toughest guys in Texas, but I would think of something. Had to.

I hit a fast trot down the creek and called out, "Pete, be brave, I'm coming to save you!"

You know, it's kind of amazing that a dog would know so much about tracks and stuff, isn't it? You bet, but in my line of work, we have to be prepared for anything. We have to be flatulent in several languages and know almost everything about tracks, prints, scents, codes and clues, the whole nine yards.

Pretty amazing, huh? You bet. Ordinary dogs need not apply.

Where were we? Oh yes, on a rescue to save Sally May's rotten little...to save a friend, a long-time friend of many years. Pete. He was in big trouble.

I had gone maybe two hundred yards when I saw something up ahead. I shut down the engines and coasted to a stop, switched on Binocular Vision and took a long, careful look. I saw...a cat! He appeared to be stalking a grasshopper.

It was Pete, I had found him! He hadn't been

eaten by coyotes and seemed to be in good shape. Sally May would be so proud!

"Hey Pete, great news, I'm here to take you home!"

I rushed forward. I didn't remember him being so large but maybe he'd picked up some pounds. Don't forget, Sally May pampered him and gave him extra scraps. That had always struck me as unfair but...real big and...he'd lost part of his tail? The coyotes must have chewed off his...a bobtail?

HUH?

I hit Full Air Brakes and slid to a stop in the sand. "Pete?"

He turned around and stared at me with yellow eyes. Big dude, real big. He had tufts of hair on both sides of his face, pointed ears, a thick body and legs, big feet. He was a cat but not the one I'd been looking for. *This wasn't Pete.*

Gulp.

He stared. My mouth was suddenly very dry. "Hi. I have a feeling we've met before, one night in the feed barn. You were looking for mice. I thought you were Pete the Barncat and jumped on your back. You, uh, beat the snot out of me."

No response, no change of expression.

"Shall I continue?" Silence. "Okay, later we

ran into each other in the Dark Unchanted Forest. You were, uh, following a friend of mine. Little Alfred, a child. Unless I'm mistaken, you're..." The breath hung in my throat. "...you're Sinister the Bobcat." Silence. "As I recall, you don't talk."

"Seldom."

"You do talk?"

"What's on your mind?"

I was surprised that he talked and surprised by his voice. I had expected it to be harsh and jagged, scary, but it was just the opposite: soft and smooth, almost refined. Somehow things didn't add up: creepy eyes, thick body, and soft voice.

I went on. "You know, I'm glad you asked, Sinister. May I call you Sinister or would you prefer Mister Bobcat?" No response, just more of those eyes. "Never mind. I'm out here in the wilderness as part of a search and rescue mission."

"Two guys horseback?"

"Yes, exactly."

"I saw them."

"Well, we got separated. I was detained, you might say, talking to a couple of buzzards."

"Always hungry?"

I laughed. "So you know Wallace and Junior?"

"Dingbats."

"Yes, they're a little strange. Anyway, I'm on a

mission to find a cousin of yours, Pete the Barncat. He wandered off and...Pete and I have been close buddies for years, yes, we go way back. You'll be interested to know that some of my best friends are cats."

He sucked at his teeth, pulled a grasshopper leg out of his mouth, looked at it, and flicked it away. "I don't get along with cats."

"Really? Well, that surprises me, I mean, you're a cat."

"I like *me*. I don't like cats."

All at once, I had a feeling that Sinister and I had things in common and might get along just fine. "I'm glad to hear you say that, Sinister, because some of my worst enemies are cats. If you ask me, they're arrogant, selfish, snooty, and can't be trusted."

"Bingo. What's the point?"

"You mean, why am I out here looking for Pete?"

"Yeah."

"Well, it's complicated. I'm doing it for Sally May."

"Who?"

"Our ranch wife. A person. For some reason, she loves her cat."

"I don't get along with people." He hosed me with those eyes. "How'd you find me?"

Uh oh. Did I dare reveal my trade secrets, that I

had tracked him down? I needed to give that some
thought, and so do you. Let's change chapters.

CHAPTER TEN

I Interrogate the Cat

Okay, there I was, out in the middle of the wilderness, interrogating a huge bobcat. "I followed some cat tracks. I thought they were Pete's."

"Wrong."

"Obviously they were yours."

"Right."

"But there was another set of tracks, suggesting the cat was being followed by coyotes."

"Yeah, they wanted a snack."

"And, well, I guess that didn't work out. I mean, you're still here."

"They left."

"They just...left?"

"I insisted."

"You insisted?"

"We had a scuffle."

"You mean a fight? You whipped two coyotes?"

"I don't get along with coyotes."

"I know, but those guys are tough."

He smiled, ever so slightly. "Not when I'm around."

His yellow stare and slinky smile made me uncomfortable, but I plunged on. "The buzzards said they saw a cat and he was limping, crippled. Was that you?"

"Yeah. Sticker."

"Sticker?"

"Paw."

"You had a sticker in your...oh great! That's what I get for taking testimony from a buzzard."

"Dingbats."

I filled my lungs with air and let it out slowly. "Sinister, you don't get along with cats, coyotes, buzzards, or people. Do you get along with anyone?"

"Chickens and quail."

"But you eat them, right?"

"Yeah."

"They're not exactly your friends."

"Not exactly."

"I guess you don't have a lot of friends."

"Yeah."

I paced a few steps away. "I was wondering about...well, dogs."

"I don't get along with dogs."

That gave me a jolt. "I hate to bring up an awkward subject but...you might have noticed that I'm a dog."

"Yeah."

"Where does that leave us?"

"I was wondering."

"I mean, I'm here and you're here and we're both here."

"One, two. Yeah."

"You seem to enjoy solitude."

"Yeah. One."

"Here's an idea. I could walk away and leave you alone."

"Wouldn't seem right."

"How come?"

"I hate dogs."

"What? Hey, you said you *didn't get along* with dogs. Now you hate us? What's happened in the last minute to turn you so bitter?"

"I was being polite."

"But Sinister, we've formed a kind of friendship."

"Very fragile."

"But we...we could work on it."

"I'm busy."

"Sinister, think about it. We could set a good example for dogs and cats in all parts of the universe. A fresh start, peace and friendship."

He studied his claws. "Boring."

"Does that mean we have to be enemies?"

"Most likely."

"So, are you talking about...a fight?"

"'Maybe so."

"A fight to the death?"

"Could be."

"So...our friendship has crumbled?"

"Yeah. Sad."

"But it's too hot for us to be warring and fighting."

He glanced up at the sun. "Pretty hot."

"We could postpone it until another day."

He shrugged. "Okay. Don't forget to show up."

"Oh yes."

"Don't be late."

"Yes sir."

He pointed his paw to the east. "Talk to Madame Moonshine, down the creek, first cave on the right."

"About Pete?"

"Whatever his name is."

He turned away from me and went back to hunting grasshoppers. I was thrilled. "Sinister, I really appreciate this. You're welcome to poach a chicken on my ranch, any time you want." Silence. "I have one last question. When you followed Little Alfred into the Dark Unchanted Forest, were you planning to eat him?"

He turned around and gave me a look that

chilled my liver. "You think I eat kids?"

"Well, I..."

"Don't leave. I've changed my mind."

"What! You mean..."

"Joking. Shut up and get out of here."

He went back to his grasshoppers and I got out of there as fast as I could. I was shaking all over. Whew!

CHAPTER ELEVEN

The Very Strange Madame Moonshine

Let me repeat myself: WHEW! I had just interviewed a huge cat who hated dogs but decided to let me go free, and he even showed a sense of humor. You add it up and you get a puzzle, a mystery, and a pretty interesting character.

Bottom Line: I had lucked out. Yes, I admit it. I had walked around the rim of a volcano and hadn't been blown to shreds. In other words, skill wasn't...although we have to admit that my personal charm might have played a role.

Yes, that needs to be factored into the equation. My intense personal charm, plus amazing interrogation techniques, had gotten me through the ordeal and luck had nothing to do with it. My interrogation had been a thunderous success and

Sinister was just lucky he hadn't tried to pull any of his Tough Guy Tricks on me, else he might have learned why I'm Head of Ranch Security and not Head of the Garbage Department.

Heh. When we look at all the evidence, things become clear.

On the other hand, I was alone in the wilderness, still looking for Sally May's cat and still had no idea where he had gone, or if he was even alive. And it was still hot.

Oh brother. I was about ready to give it up and admit defeat when an idea lit up the broad sky of my mind, and we're talking about fireworks.

MADAME MOONSHINE!

Remember MM? She was a witchy little owl with secret powers and I had done business with her on several occasions. She had cured me of the dreaded disease, Eye-Crosserosis, and had helped me out of several tough situations.

Madame Moonshine was a little weird...no, she was seriously weird, but she'd helped me before and maybe she could help me now. And you know what else? I knew where she lived (in a cave) and I just happened to be close to it.

Brilliant idea. I don't know why I hadn't thought of it sooner. Wow.

I picked up the pace and threaded my way

through the tamaracks and willows along the creek and kept a close eye on the south bank. Then...there it was, the cave. I climbed up the incline and reached the entrance.

There, to my surprise, I saw note, a piece of paper, pinned onto the dirt with a mesquite thorn. Something was written on it. I glanced around to see if I was being watched (no), then read the mysterious message. You want to look at it? I guess it wouldn't hurt.

Dear Hank the Rabbit:

You've reached the voicemail of Madame Moonshine, Professional Owl. I'm away from the office...or maybe I'm not, it's hard to say, but I've been expecting you for weeks, where have you been?

Please come in and make yourself comfortable. I'll be back, when and if I decide to return, if I've left at all. I've made you a cup of tea. Do you take sugar? Never mind. I've already given you sugar or I haven't, you will find out soon enough.

Timothy, my bodyguard, will be blocking the entrance. I'm sure you remember him. You will have to give him a pass code. Today's code is SCRAM, all capital letters. No, that can't be right. That was yesterday's code.

What day is today? Today is the day before tomorrow, two days after yesterday, and we change the code every month. Isn't this fun?

Today's code is BuZzOfF, with alternating capital and small letters. Upon hearing the code, Timothy will open the outer doors...unless he's feeling cheeky, in which case he will bite you and inject two pints of rattlesnake venom. No, wait, he has a toothache. Never mind.

Toodle-do and see you soon...maybe.
MM

Well, that message confirmed everything I knew about Madame Moonshine. She was extremely odd, and that's putting it nicely.

I stuck my head into the cave. "Hello? Madame?" After a moment of silence, I heard a buzzing sound that raised the hair along my backbone. It sounded a lot like, well, the buzzing of a rattlesnake. Then I saw him: Big Tim, a six-foot diamondback rattlesnake, with his ugly head poised above the coils of his body. His wicked eyes bored into me and he was flicking out his tongue.

My mouth went dry. "Hey, Tim, how's it going, buddy?" The buzzing grew louder and he appeared ready to strike. "Oh, the code word. You want the code, right? Let me think. Oh yes, here it is: *SCRAM, all capital letters.*" More buzzing, more threatening eyes. "Wait, that was yesterday's code. Here's the new one: *BuZzOfF, with alternating capital and small letters.*"

It worked! The ugliest snake in Texas melted away and slithered out of the entrance. I struggled to catch a breath. "Thanks, pal, I'll go inside, if that's okay." Whew! I almost fainted.

I crawled into the narrow opening and found myself in a large room, Madame's office or home or whatever she called it. It was dark at first but my eyes adjusted and...there she was, lying on a platform with her head propped on one wing, staring at me with big full-moon eyes.

She spoke. "Oh my goodness, unless my eyes deceive me, it's Hank the Rabbit! You made it past the Five Ordeals."

"Well, I saw only one ordeal, your snake."

"The other four are so terrifying, we don't show them, but you survived and you're here. You're such a clever rabbit!"

"Uh...Madame, I've said this before...

"And you shan't say it again. You insist you're not a rabbit but I insist you are, therefore you will be, whether you are or not. Have some tea, O Rabbity Hank." I searched the room. There

94

wasn't any tea. She sat up and glanced around, swiveling her head the way owls do. "Someone forgot to make the tea. What day is this?"

"I don't know, Monday, I guess."

"No, Monday was two weeks ago. Today is Someday and tomorrow is Glumday and we expected you two weeks ago last March. Where oh where have you been?"

"How could you have expected me two weeks ago?"

"Simple. How does a rabbit know how to hop?"

"I have no idea."

"Then I shall explain." She rolled her eyes to the ceiling. "First, the rabbit hopes, then we remove the E from hope. What does that leave?"

"Uh...let me think. Mope?"

She gave me a ferocious look. "No! Hope – E = what?"

"Oh, I see now. Mop. That was easy."

Her eyes flashed and she screeched, "No, no, no! Naughty rabbit, naughty rabbit! When you remove the E from hope, you get HOP, not mop." She heaved a heavy sigh. "This will require a song. Please pay attention." And with that, she launched into a song.

How Did the Rabbit Learn How to Hop?

How did the rabbit learn how to hop?
Not easy but greasy and grim.
You start with HOPE which rhymes with a rope
That's limp and squeezy and thin.

Birds are absurd and rabbits have habits
And habits are harder to bloom.
Transition from hoping to hopping takes time
And a trip to the surgery room.

With a scalpel, you make a tiny incision
And probe inside the word.
It has four little letters and ends with an E
That's silent and never is heard.

With tweezers and scissors you enter the word
And snip off the E with a chop.
You remove the letter and suture the slice,
And what remains ...is HOP!

Ye rabbits of the world, take heed and rejoice.
Don't allow your hop to flop.
You now have method for hopping down the road
And it doesn't involve a mop. Repeat,
It has nothing to do with a mop.
This nonsense...must stop!

She finished the song and looked at me. "Now do you understand?"

I lied. "Oh, yes ma'am, it's all clear now."

"Good. Stop the mop. We can only hope to stope the mope on tope of the rock and hop. That is what rabbits are supposed to do. First they hope, then they hop. You should know that, you mop. Why why do I have to have to repeat repeat myself self?"

"I'm hearing an echo."

"No, you're hearing an *owlco*. Owls prowl and howl and scowl, and I can assure you, O Rabbity Hank, there is no hope in a mope or hop in a mop. Am I making myself clear?"

"Oh you bet, I've got it now." I had no idea what she'd just said.

"Good." She looked at her wing as though it were a note pad. "We had you scheduled for two weeks ago. You missed your appointment."

"Madame, two weeks ago, none of this was happening."

"You just weren't aware of it, but never mind. You're finally here and what is it that you want?"

At last, we'd gotten down to the business. Keep reading.

CHAPTER TWELVE

Amazing.
Incredible.

Okay, there we were in Madame Moonshine's cave. I gave her the story: the cat had been missing for two days, Sally May was very concerned, and I was on a rescue mission to find him.

Madame rubbed her chin with the tip of her wing. "Nothing fits together. 'Cat' doesn't rhyme with hop, mop, hope, or mope. Are you sure it was a cat, not a bat or a fat rat?"

"I'm very sure. Pete is 100% cat, in the worst sense of the word."

"Not a mouse, a house, or a louse?"

"No ma'am."

"Hmmm. Let me consult." She closed her eyes and lifted a wing.

"O power, power, sweet and sour,
Hoping hop and moping mop.
Give to me a vision that
Will find this silly wayward cat."

There was a moment of eerie silence, then her eyes popped open. "Your cat didn't run away."

"He's not my cat. I don't even like him, but two days ago, he vanished."

"Vanished is only what you can't see. Vanished...famished...banished. Let me check." Again, she closed her eyes and raised a wing.

"O vapors, vapors, vanilla wafers,
Endless prairie, lonesome city.
Vanished famished banished soul
Where is the missing kitty-kitty?"

This time, she got a bigger response, a bang and a puff of smoke. Her eyes popped open. "Your cat is close to home, in a dark place. He needs your help."

"Okay, good. Maybe I can get this mess cleaned up. Where is he?"

She rolled her eyes up to the ceiling. "That part was garbled, but it sounded like 'Mule's Head.'"

"Mule's Head? That's all?"

Her gaze drifted down to me. "You were two weeks late for your appointment. You're lucky to get anything."

"Madame, nothing sounds like 'Mule's Head.'"

"Well, don't blame me. It's not my cat." She gave me a little smile. "Here's a thought. Why don't you stay for the winter? We could drink tea and make up rhymes. It might be fun."

I rose to my feet. "Thanks, Madame, but I need to get this case wrapped up. Don't forget, I'm Head of Ranch Security."

Her face became very solemn. "Oh yes. Sh-h-h. We mustn't disturb the great mind at work. Sh-h-h."

"Exactly, but I appreciate your help, I really do."

"Goodbye, O Rabbity Hank, and try not to agitate my snake. He's had a toothache and shouldn't be biting anyone."

"Yes ma'am, bye now." I headed for the cave door. Big Tim was coiled up and looking sour. "Excuse me. I hope your toothache gets better." He stuck out his tongue and rolled out of the way. "Don't step on that tongue."

Hee hee. I love putting a stinger on a snake.

I dived out into the sunlight and grabbed a big gulp of fresh air. Gag, it was hot but I kicked up the jets and headed for Home Base. All the way,

I kept repeating Madame Moonshine's mysterious clue: "Mule's Head. Mule's Head." What could those two words possibly mean? Fool's Bread? Stool's Bed? Cruel Ned?

Nothing fit, nothing worked, and it was burning up the wires in my brain.

Ten minutes later, I roared into headquarters, made a smooth landing, and went straight to the machine shed. I had some unfinished business to take care of.

"Drover, report to the front!"

Silence, then a faint voice. "I'm not here. I'm at the office."

"Drover, it's been a long day. I'm not in the mood for your foolishness. Report to the front immediately."

"Oh drat." A moment later, he appeared. "How'd you know I was here?"

"Never mind, stand up straight. This court martial is in session and we find you guilty of all charges."

"Gosh, what did I do?"

"Everything. You will stand with your nose in the corner for weeks. March!"

"Oh drat."

I marched the little slacker to his prison cell and parked his nose in the corner. He asked if I'd found Pete.

"No, but I found Madame Moonshine and she gave me some clues. Number one, Pete's not lost in the pasture because he never left headquarters."

"I'll be derned. I wonder where he could be."

"Keep your nose in the corner. Number two, she didn't give a location, just two mysterious words that sound like where he is. It must be some kind of secret code."

"Can I get a drink?"

"No. You can't get a drink or go to the bathroom or eat or sleep. Your nose stays in the corner."

"It hurts my neck."

"Nobody cares." I began pacing. "This one has me stumped. Wherever Pete is sounds like 'Mule's Head'."

He gave me a silly grin. "Oh, that's easy."

I whirled around. "It's *not* easy. I've already told you that it's an uncrackable secret code. And put your nose back in the corner."

"It's easy, no fooling. TOOL SHED."

I stared at the runt. "That's the most ridiculous..."

"Don't you get it? 'Tool Shed' sounds like 'Mule's Head'. Pete got locked in the tool shed, hee hee. Are you proud of me?"

My head was spinning. Tool Shed. If it was so easy, why hadn't I thought of it?

I faced him with a look of steel. "Drover, I've decided to suspend your sentence, but you must never discuss this conversation with anyone, do you understand? If word of this ever leaked out, it could have a terrible effect on the morale of this unit. All of us in the Security Division are sworn to silence."

"My neck feels better. Thanks."

I hit Turbo Five and went roaring down to the yard gate. There, I established a Forward Position and began pumping out some barks, big ones. "Sally May, you need to come outside at once! Repeat: come at once, I have important news about your cat, over."

At last the back door opened and I saw her face. Oops, she looked...well, she didn't look like a lady who was about to receive good news.

She closed the door. How could I give her good news if...the door opened again. She stepped out on the porch. She was carrying Baby Molly on her hip. She came down the sidewalk, holding me in a steady gaze.

At the gate, she stopped. "Is this something important?"

Yes ma'am, very important.

She gave her head a nod and came out the gate. See? I told you she had radar.

I went streaking up the hill and had to wait

for her to catch up. I mean, she was wearing flip-flop shoes and packing a child. I went straight to the tool shed, an old outhouse that had been moved, painted green, and converted into a shed where she stored her garden tools.

I pointed my nose toward the door, and we're talking about a flaming arrow. She said, "You think..." Her eyes rolled upward and she gasped, "Oh my stars, of course! I was putting away my tools." She unlatched the door and threw it open. Sunlight spilled inside and revealed...HER CAT.

He sat up, blinked his eyes, and yawned. "My goodness, the cops are here. Hankie, what took you so long?"

Sally May was beside herself. Somehow she managed to hang on to Molly with one hand and scoop up the cat with the other. She hugged him and nuzzled his face, while Pete rubbed and purred.

Then she turned a pair of sparkling eyes on me. "Hank, bless your heart, thank you!"

Wow. Those were words I'd seldom heard, and it got even better. She invited me into her house and fed me two raw eggs with milk. Then she gave me a good brushing and pulled the sand burs out of my hair.

That's where I was around five o'clock when Loper and Slim returned to give Sally May the

sad news that they hadn't found her cat...and found him sitting in the iris patch. That produced a mixed response, shall we say. Naturally, they were glad to see Kitty alive but more than a little hacked that they had wasted half a day looking for him. But Sally May was happy and that was the whole point.

She led me to the yard gate, gave me one last pat on the head, and went back inside. Then I heard a voice. "Pssst! Hankie?" It was the cat.

Here he came, out of the iris patch, slithering along with his tail stuck straight in the air and rubbing his way down the fence. He sat down and looked at me through the hog-wire fence.

"Yes? You called?"

"Hankie, you've put me in an awkward position and I don't appreciate it, only I do appreciate it."

"What is that supposed to mean?"

"Well," he looked up at the sky, "you did me a favor. Until I balance the score, my life is upside-down." He leaned toward me and whispered, "I'll have to be nice."

"Forget about it. It was just an accident."

"No, no, Hankie, there's no forgetting. It's been recorded in the Great Book of Life. The question is—do you want to share the rest of your days with a cat who's NICE all the time? I'd be miserable...and so would you."

That gave me a shock. "You'd actually do that?"

"It's bigger than both of us, Hankie, beyond our control."

I paced a few steps away, then turned and faced him. "How do we get out of this?"

He sighed. "I'll have to return the favor, Hankie, so please think of something."

"I can't think of...wait a second." I paced back to him and told him the whole story about the Sleeping Powder Poisoning Episode. "See, if you had played a dirty trick, it would explain why Drover and I were sleeping during business hours. We'd be off the hook for slacking on the job."

"How interesting."

"But it won't work, Pete. You couldn't have done it, you were locked in the shed."

He began twitching the last three inches of his tail. "Hankie, what would you say if I told you that I *did* do it?"

"I wouldn't believe you. How could you have done it?"

He grinned. "What would you say if I told you that there was a secret trap door in the tool shed? And what would you say if I told you that I slipped out the door and sprinkled Sleeping Powder all over your office?"

"I'd say...if there was a trap door and you really slipped outside, why did you go back into the tool shed?"

He snickered. "Oh Hankie, you just don't get it. I'm a cat! For two whole days, everyone on the ranch was thinking about...ME! They were distraught, in tears. It was delicious."

Bingo. I had him! We had a crime and a motive. I had wrung a confession out of the little sneak and had blown the case wide open. "Pete, you're despicable."

"I know, Hankie, and now the score is back to zero."

"Right, no more Nice Doggie. How would you like to climb a tree?"

He blinked his weird kitty eyes. "You know, Hankie, if I were you, I'd wait until tomorrow. You might as well enjoy a few hours of peace with Sally May."

"Don't tell me what to do. Okay, first thing in the morning, it's war."

"Happy days are here again...and your mother's a toad."

"Oh yeah? Your mother's a fat hog."

"I hope you get fleas."

"I hope you get 235 bedbugs." I whirled away and marched down to the Security Division's Vast

Office Complex, tingling all over with the sheer joy of winning another huge moral victory over the cat.

Wow, I was off the hook for sleeping on the job! I had solved the case, humbled the cat, and become a hero to Our Beloved Ranch Wife. And tomorrow, Kitty and I would resume our lousy relationship and our lives would return to normal.

Does it get any better than that? Not around here. This case is...wait a second. What if Pete made up that story about the trap door? I mean, cats lie, they'd rather tell a fib than...never mind, it's too complicated.

This case is CLOSED, and don't ask any questions.

Have you read all of Hank's adventures?

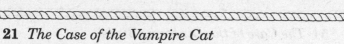

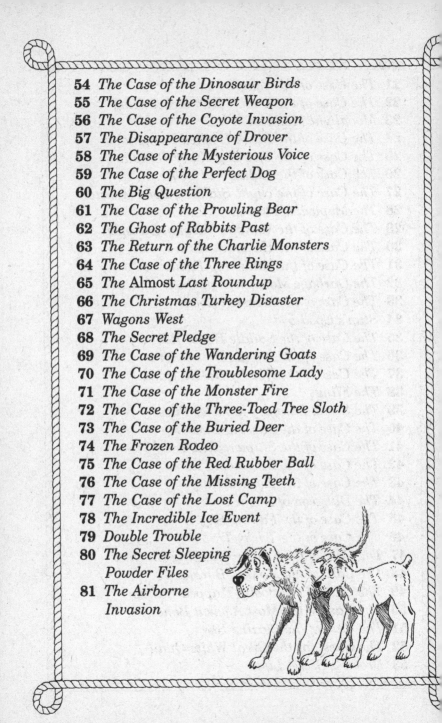

Finding Hank

The Most-Often Asked Questions about Hank the Cowdog

For more than 35 years, John R. Erickson has entertained three generations of readers with Hank the Cowdog's hilarious antics, and now, for the first time, in this beautiful, full-color volume, he answers the most common questions he has received from fans over the years!

Written in an engaging question-and answer style, this collector's item — complete with illustrations and original photographs — provides a unique behind-the-scenes look at the people, places, and real-life animals and incidents behind your favorite Hank stories!

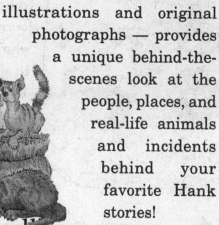

Confessions of a Cowdog

READ THE SHORT STORIES THAT STARTED IT ALL!

Believe it or not, once upon a time Hank the Cowdog was just *one* of many endearing characters who made their debut in an early collection of short-stories by beloved Texas author, John R. Erickson. First published under the title, *The Devil in Texas*, Erickson compiled his funniest fiction writings and released this book to his local ranching community. Inspired by the encouragement he received, he later developed one particular character, Hank the Cowdog, who quickly became

a literary hero in his own right. And, if you love Hank, you're in for a treat! In these stories, you'll get inside the head of an ornery bronc who's about to be saddle-broke, read the journal of a spunky ranch wife who has to find creative ways to get the cowboys to help her around the homestead, and gain some comical insights into what a cowboy's work really involves—the *unglamorous* side!

And, be sure to check out the Audiobooks!

If you've never heard a *Hank the Cowdog* audiobook, you're missing out on a lot of fun! Each Hank book has also been recorded as an unabridged audiobook for the whole family to enjoy!

Praise for the Hank Audiobooks:

"It's about time the Lone Star State stopped hogging Hank the Cowdog, the hilarious adventure series about a crime solving ranch dog. Ostensibly for children, the audio renditions by author John R. Erickson are sure to build a cult following among adults as well." — *Parade Magazine*

"Full of regional humor . . . vocals are suitably poignant and ridiculous. A wonderful yarn." — *Booklist*

"For the detectin' and protectin' exploits of the canine Mike Hammer, hang Hank's name right up there with those of other anthropomorphic greats...But there's no sentimentality in Hank: he's just plain more rip-roaring fun than the others. Hank's misadventures as head of ranch security on a spread somewhere in the Texas Panhandle are marvelous situation comedy." — *School Library Journal*

"Knee-slapping funny and gets kids reading."

— *Fort Worth Star Telegram*

Love Hank's Hilarious Songs?

Hank the Cowdog's "Greatest Hits" albums bring together the music from the unabridged audiobooks you know and love! These wonderful collections of hilarious (and sometimes touching) songs are unmatched. Where else can you learn about coyote philosophy, buzzard lore, why your dog is protecting an old corncob, how bugs compare to hot dog buns, and much more!

And, be sure to visit Hank's "Music Page" on the official website to listen to some of the songs and download FREE Hank the Cowdog ringtones!

The Ranch Life Learning Series

Want to learn more about ranching? Check out Hank's hilarious and educational new series, Ranch Life Learning, brought to you by Maverick Books and The National Ranching Heritage Center!

Saddle up for some fun as the same cast of characters you've come to know and love in the Hank the Cowdog series gives you a first-class introduction to life on a ranch!

In these books, you'll learn things like: the difference between a ranch and a farm, how cows digest grass, what it takes to run a ranch as a successful business, how to take care of cattle throughout the various seasons, what the daily life of a working cowboy looks like, qualities to look for in a good horse, the many kinds of wild animals you might see if you spent a few days on Hank's ranch, the tremendous impact different kinds of weather have on every aspect of ranching, and, last but not least, the consequences and benefits of wildfires!

"Audio-Only" Stories

Ever wondered what those "Audio-Only" Stories in Hank's Official Store are all about?

The Audio-Only Stories are Hank the Cowdog adventures that have never been released as books. They are about half the length of a typical Hank book, and there are currently seven of them. They have run as serial stories in newspapers for years and are now available as audiobooks!

We all know Hank loves to eat ... and now *you* can try some of his favorite recipes!

Have you visited
Sally May's Kitchen yet?

http://www.hankthecowdog.com/recipes

Here, you'll find recipes for:

Sally May's Apple Pie

Hank's Picante Sauce

Round-Up Green Beans

Little Alfred's and Baby Molly's Favorite Cookies

Cowboy Hamburgers with Gravy

Chicken-Ham Casserole

...and MORE!

Have you visited Hank's official website yet?

www.hankthecowdog.com

Don't miss out on exciting *Hank the Cowdog* games and activities, as well as up-to-date news about upcoming books in the series!

When you visit, you'll find:

- Hank's BLOG, which is the first place we announce upcoming books and new products!
- Hank's Official Shop, with tons of great *Hank the Cowdog* books, audiobooks, games, t-shirts, stuffed animals, mugs, bags, and more!
- Links to Hank's social media, whereby Hank sends out his "Cowdog Wisdom" to fans.
- A FREE, printable "Map of Hank's Ranch"!
- Hank's Music Page where you can listen to songs and even download FREE ringtones!
- A way to sign up for Hank's free email updates
- Sally May's "Ranch Roundup Recipes"!
- Printable & Colorable Greeting Cards for Holidays.

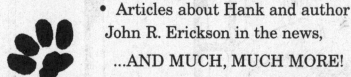

- Articles about Hank and author John R. Erickson in the news,

...AND MUCH, MUCH MORE!

search the website GO

BOOKS
The Collection

FAN ZONE
Fun & Games

AUTHOR
Meet the Creator

STORE
Books & More

Find Toys, Games, Books & More
at the Hank shop.

ANNOUNCING: A sneak peek at Hank #66

Hank Plays Cupid:

GAMES
COME PLAY WITH HANK & PALS

BOOKS
BROWSE THE ENTIRE HANK CATALOG

FRIENDS
GET TO KNOW THE RANCH GANG

 Visit Hank's Facebook page

 Follow Hank on Twitter

Watch Hank on YouTube

 Follow Hank on Pinterest

Send Hank an Email

FROM THE BLOG

JAN 26 Hank is Cupid in Disguise...

JAN 13 The Valentine's Day Robbery! - a Snippet from the Story

DEC 04 Getting SIGNED Hank the Cowdog books for Christmas!

OCT 14 Education Association's lists of recommended books?

VISIT THE BLOG

Hank's Survey
We'd love to know what you think! GO

TEACHER'S CORNER

Download fun activity guides, discussion questions and more.

SALLY MAY'S RECIPES

Discover delicious recipes from Sally May herself. GO

Hank's Music.
Free ringtones, music and more!

MORE

Official Shop
Find books, audio, toys and more!

LET'S GO

Join Hank's Security Force
Get the activity letter and other cool stuff.

JOIN SECURITY FORCE

Get the Latest

Keep up with Hank's news and promotions by signing up for our e-news.

Looking for The Hank Times fan club newsletter?

Enter your email address   SIGN UP

Hank in the News

Find out what the media is saying about Hank. GO

FEATURED BOOK

The Christmas Turkey Disaster

Now Available!

Hank is in real trouble this time. I..

BUY   READ   LISTEN

BOOKS
Browse Titles
Buy Books
Audio Sampler

FAN ZONE
Games
Hank & Friends
Security Force

AUTHOR
John Erickson's Bio
Hank in the News
In Concert

SHOP
The Books
Store
Get Help

Teacher's Corner

Know a teacher who uses Hank in their classroom? You'll want to be sure they know about Hank's "Teacher's Corner"! Just click on the link on the homepage, and you'll find free teacher's aids, such as a printable map of Hank's ranch, a reading log, coloring pages, blog posts specifically for teachers and librarians, quizzes and much more!

The following activities are samples from *The Hank Times*, the official newspaper of Hank's Security Force. Please do not write on these pages unless this is your book. And, even then, why not just find a scrap of paper?

"Photogenic"
Memory Quiz

We all know that Hank has a "photogenic" memory—being aware of your surroundings is an important quality for a Head of Ranch Security. Now *you* can test your powers of observation.

How good is your memory? Look at the illustration on page 19 and try to remember as many things about it as possible. Then turn back to this page and see how many questions you can answer.

1. Was Hank looking Straight Ahead, Up or Down?

2. Was Slim holding the bucket in HIS Left or Right hand?

3. How many clouds were there?
   2, 3, 4, or 5?

4. Was Slim holding a hammer, screwdriver, or wrench?

5. How many ears could you see?
   2, 3, 4, or 16?

"Word Maker"

Try making up to twenty words from the letters in the names below. Use as many letters as possible. However, don't just add an "s" to a word you've already listed in order to have it count as another. Try to make up entirely new words for each line!

Then, count the total number of letters used in all of the words you made, and see how well you did using the Security Force Rankings below!

MOONSHINE PETE

_____   _____

_____   _____

_____   _____

_____   _____

_____   _____

_____   _____

_____   _____

_____   _____

_____   _____

_____   _____

66 - 70   You spend too much time with J.T. Cluck and the chickens.

71 - 73   You are showing some real Security Force potential.

74 - 75   You have earned a spot on our Ranch Security team.

76 +   Wow! You rank up there as a top-of-the-line cowdog.

Yard Gate

The Yard Gate is a busy place on the ranch. Scrap Time is definitely one of Hank's favorite events. However, there are characters coming and going at all times at the yard gate. Let's go through the clues below and see if we can figure out in what order the characters below made an appearance at the Yard Gate. Good Luck!

Clues:

Species arrive together

Longer names first

Early birds get the worms (scraps too!)

1. _____

2. _____

3. _____

4. _____

5. _____

JUNIOR

WALLACE

DROVER

HANK

PETE

"Rhyme Time"

If Madame Moonshine were to leave Twitchell, what kinds of jobs do you think she could find? Make a rhyme using "Moonshine" that would relate to her new job possibilities.

Example: Madame Moonshine gets a job making sure people don't cut while waiting to see a movie.

Answer: Moonshine **LINE.**

1. Madame Moonshine gets a job complaining about everything!

2. Madame Moonshine opens a restaurant.

3. Madame Moonshine opens a store that is known for selling very good products.

4. Madame Moonshine becomes a chiropractor.

5. Madame Moonshine becomes a script prompter, helping actors remember what to say.

6. Madame Moonshine opens a Christmas tree business.

7. Madame Moonshine discovers a cave that is filled with gold!

Answers:

John R. Erickson,

a former cowboy, has written numerous books for both children and adults and is best known for his acclaimed *Hank the Cowdog* series. The *Hank* series began as a self-publishing venture in Erickson's garage in 1982 and has endured to become one of the nation's most popular series for children and families.

Through the eyes of Hank the Cowdog, a smelly, smart-aleck Head of Ranch Security, Erickson gives readers a glimpse into daily life on a cattle ranch in the West Texas Panhandle. His stories have won a number of awards, including the Audie, Oppenheimer, Wrangler, and Lamplighter Awards, and have been translated into Spanish, Danish, Farsi, and Chinese. In 2019, Erickson was inducted into the Texas Literary Hall of Fame. *USA Today* calls the *Hank the Cowdog* books "the best family entertainment in years." Erickson lives and works on his ranch in Perryton, Texas, with his family.

Nicolette G. Earley

was born and raised in the Texas Hill Country. She began working for Maverick Books in 2008, editing, designing new Hank the Cowdog books, and working with the artist who had put faces on all the characters: Gerald Holmes. When Holmes died in 2019, she discovered that she could reproduce his drawing style and auditioned for the job. She made her debut appearance in Book 75, illustrating new books in the series she read as a child. She and her husband, Keith, and their children live in the Texas hill country.